Love
and Other
Possibilities

PARTHIAN

Love

and
Other Possibilities

Lewis Davies

PARTHIAN

Parthian
The Old Surgery
Napier Street
Cardigan
SA43 1ED
www.parthianbooks.co.uk

First published in 2008
New edition 2009
© Lewis Davies
All Rights Reserved

ISBN 978-1-906998-08-0

The publisher acknowledges the financial support of the Welsh
Books Council.

Cover photograph: Tivoli Gardens, Summer 2008 © Tai Griffiths
Cover design: www.theundercard.co.uk
Typeset by logodædaly

Printed and bound by Gomer Press, Llandysul, Wales

FT Pbk

British Library Cataloguing in Publication Data

A cataloguing record for this book is available from the British
Library.

Stories

Mr Roopratna's Chocolate

Mr Roopratna brushed leaves in the Palm Garden. He must have been working when I arrived to take the bungalow. Three rooms, two I didn't need and a kitchen. I checked the locks on the windows, then the water running from the shower. It dribbled out, warm and salty.

'It is better in the evening.' De Silva cut a wide white smile. 'Now it's the dry months, low pressure in the afternoon.'

It was cheap; the village was sliding into the off season and the stream of German tourists had also dropped to a trickle as the monsoon gathered patiently out in the ocean.

'There's a good gardener, very good.' He nodded to make sure I understood.

Mr Roopratna was waiting in the darkness of the verandah when I returned from a bar at the beach. The sun had dipped quickly under the sea, flooding the jungle in a deep whispering night of bats and cicadas high in the trees. He bowed reverently and pointed to the door. His lips opened quickly, enunciating a request in a burst of unfamiliar words.

I pointed towards the bungalow, and he nodded in agreement, his eyes gleaming when I switched on a light which flickered uneasily in bursts of low current. Brown skin was stretched taut across a thin face, shining where hair thinned to wisps of grey on his scalp. His chest was bare, and faded grey trousers rose from his calves to be secured at his waist with a black leather belt.

'You're the gardener.'

He nodded vigorously.

I offered my hand which he shook very shyly; then he stood still, only returning my smile.

'Can I help you?'

He pointed at the light switch and then further into the bungalow where the corridor twisted back to the bedrooms.

'Rooms yes, light?'

He nodded again and pointed. Then moved a few steps into the wide, open kitchen beckoning me to follow him. His feet, bare and calloused, echoed faintly in the hollow stillness of the bungalow, barely glancing the ochre tiles on the floor.

At the back of the bungalow, where the bathroom edged into the jungle, he pointed to a door I had not seen when I had first been shown the rooms. It was locked from the outside.

Mr Roopratna flicked a light switch on the wall, quickly bowed and retreated from the entrance.

I looked through one of the cracks in the planed wooden door to the room beyond. A sink, a few tattered shelves and a palm mat on the floor. I pulled away sharply as Mr Roopratna shuffled in from his own side entrance.

I retreated back to my own room. I had not been expecting to share the bungalow. I thought about the stranger in the next room as the fan stirred listlessly below the ceiling, brushing the brittle mesh of the mosquito net against my skin.

The first weeks drifted easily. I stretched out wide canvasses under the verandah and painted the hanging fronds of palm trees and quick lithe motions of children as they climbed down from the village on the hill to collect water from the deep, clear well in the garden.

I liked to imagine I was working hard, rising at seven to catch the thick early light that dripped in through the trees from the east. But Mr Roopratna was always working earlier, brushing leaves from the weeping trees into tidy piles. Moving slowly, he cornered each one with the constant trush, trush of his brushing, corralling them into corners. The leaves played with him, teasing his time, and by the following morning a new flock would have settled, and he would resume his journey around the wide, tree-filled garden.

In the afternoons I read, the heavy heat of a thickening monsoon congealing the life of the garden until even the roller singing from the high branches of a jackfruit tree fell silent.

Mr Roopratna would retreat to the shade of the coconut palms and deliberately sharpen the blade of a scythe or just sit, eyes half closed, rocking gently.

He began speaking to me on the third morning when I practised my newly learned words of Sinhalese, strange sounds that stuttered uncomfortably across my tongue. He understood them in a broad, surprised smile and replied in a long monologue that left me smiling for minutes while he leaned on his brush, talking freely and pointing.

I tried to paint his movements, but he had a grace that frustrated before finally defeating my clumsy efforts. His arms and legs seemed to move without strain through the turgid heat, while my own smudged their form upon a succession of abandoned canvasses.

He came to see a third attempt when he realised I was watching his progress. His face drew to a grin which he stifled to a serious nod.

In the evenings he began to sit in the light of the verandah talking quietly to himself, while I continued with the books I used to shorten the night. He wouldn't drink the beer I offered him but liked the expensive chocolate I bought from the Oriental Hotel, treating each square as the rarest of luxuries.

Geckos, pale to the walls, watched us as I plotted progress.

But the canvasses were not shaping as I wanted them. The oil was drying too fast and I couldn't mix the deep greens that merged with the forest.

At the end of the first month De Silva arrived by rickshaw to collect his rent. He was a large, genial man whose expansive gestures emphasised his natural generosity.

'Are you sure you can afford to pay? Pay me next week, perhaps you have more money then?'

He accepted a glass of arrack and relaxed into one of his own rattan chairs.

'Perhaps you take the house for six months? No?'

I shook my head.

'I think you like it here, you work well, you're a painter yes?'

I nodded my agreement despite my stubborn canvasses.

We drank further from the arrack. It was a thin golden alcohol that climbed into my head quickly.

'The gardener, he speaks to me in the mornings.'

De Silva laughed easily.

'He is a good man, you don't worry about him.'

'No, not worried, just can't understand what he says. He speaks no English.'

'He talks about his sons; they are in the Navy at Trinco.'

'His sons?'

'Yes, and about sweeping the leaves at Buckingham Palace. He thinks he sweeps leaves for the Queen of England.' He waved his arms to indicate his garden. 'She would like it here I think.'

Another week meandered. Mr Roopratna corralled more leaves and continued to talk to me in the mornings. I learned the words for sons out of my phrase book, and his smile, never far below the surface, broadened with a deep pride. From his room he brought a smudged black and white photograph of two dark boys spruced clean in uniform at a parade.

'Trinco.' He pointed east, Matara side.

'Are you from Trinco?'

He nodded in agreement, but De Silva claimed he was from a village twenty miles along the south coast, Badulla side. Trinco was two hundred miles away on the east.

He held the photograph proudly as he pointed to the sailors, then to his own chest.

'Fine sons.' My language extended to little more. Mr Roopratna put the photograph away.

The following week De Silva arrived with a bag full of house paints and a little girl he introduced as his daughter. The girl was shy and twisted around behind her father's legs to hide from the white stranger.

'For you, yes?' He pointed at the paints, opening the bag to reveal bright reds, yellows and greens in litre tins.

'House paints.'

'Yes, yes.' He guided me enthusiastically into the bungalow. A wide white wall dominated the room. 'A painting here.'

I retreated from the wall.

'Er, I paint, er people, trees.'

'Yes, here. The big hotels in Hikkaduwa, they all have wall paintings, you paint here?' The wall pushed out: white. 'Trees and people.'

His daughter whispered to him in Sinhalese, and he swung her up into his arms.

'She says she would like elephants in it, like at Kandy.'

He refused the arrack, looking down to his daughter for explanation, but stayed to discuss his plans for the Palm Garden. There was room for another bungalow in the corner where he had planted a string of stubborn banana plants that had refused to flourish as he had expected.

'I think the soil poor there, too much salt.'

The village was twisting itself further to the requirements of wealthy Germans and Swiss escaping the European winter with a crop of new hotels rising slowly just beyond the fringe of the lagoon.

'This year was good but next year who knows? I build this and no one comes. I think the troubles will start again, then everything quiet.'

'You think the peace will break?'

'We are waiting now, they do not talk anymore, and when they do it is just words.'

He looked around for the young girl.

'Bandi?'

9

She came running from the garden clutching a crimson flower Mr Roopratna had given her.

I enjoyed painting the mural. It was the first thing that had come easily for five months. I mixed the green darker, colouring a thick luxuriant jungle with a river plunging into a waterfall before bursting out onto a plain filled with elephants. Monkeys hung from the trees, cheerful and human. It was a long way from my canvasses of vague brushed expressionism.

Mr Roopratna watched me for longer now as I daubed the white wall into colour. Gasps of admiration had greeted my big brown elephants, and he spoke the word *Wandura* when the monkeys appeared, then pointed out to the jackfruit tree where a troop sometimes settled in the late evening to feast.

The painting was a success. Mr Roopratna called a band of children who had come down to drag water from the well into the doorway to view the scene. They whispered to themselves, pointing to the wall before edging back with faint apologies when I invited them closer.

He also asked to borrow my radio, which I used to remind me of the world beyond. Things I could remember about the news and strange, unusual reports from Singapore and Dacca as private tragedies became public entertainment.

He listened to it in the afternoon, earnestly trying to find a frequency that would talk to him, a blur of light, faraway language carrying over from beneath the palms.

'It is very good.'

De Silva was delighted with the mural. He edged up closer, a critic dissecting the work.

'Many colours.'

Its fame spread quickly and within a week I had three commissions from the village on the hill. Another forest scene, Buddha and a leopard for the school. I was paid with food: coconuts, boiled jack and a bag full of freshly dried cashews.

Mr Roopratna proudly led me down to the Hotel Ocean for a fourth. He talked volubly to a young waiter who had joined him for the performance.

I was enjoying the work and gave up my canvasses completely, preferring to fish from the headland in the early morning. Mullet drifted through the clear water, teasing me with their ignorance of my hook, while fishermen in short wooden catamarans waved as they skirted the shallows.

I take a week to travel north into the hill country. Paddybirds fly low over the water scattering reflections that flap through the rippled surface of narrow lakes fringing the coast road.

Further north a crowded bus twists through a jungle thick with people. At each town the bus is surrounded by children selling peanuts and chewing gum. Their

11

brown faces smile expectantly at my white one, inspired by the novelty and hope of an easy sale.

A man selling shoes and speaking fluent English shares my seat as far as Wellawaya. He talks briefly of the war.

'It is bad. They ask too much. One half of the country. It is too much. We will have to defeat them.'

His shoes are shiny patent red and black in imitation leather.

'I have a friend in Germany. He writes to me every year. Good friend.'

He picks out a colour Polaroid of a big German with a huge, smiling moustache from his wallet.

'Business partner. One day I go to Germany. Very good country. No troubles there.'

At Ella I wait out a few days, drinking tea looking down over the stubby bushes which pattern the hills to the plains far below. The air is fresher than the thick shimmering heat of the plains. In the evening I wait for the blink of a lighthouse a hundred miles away on the coast at Matara, reminding me of the Palm Garden. The afternoons drift. I spend a few hours hitching down to a waterfall on the road a thousand feet below. A quick swim in the plunge pool, then a slow, sweet journey back up in the cab of a lorry, two men delivering sugar into the hill country from south of Wellawaya. Strong sweet smells of the newly refined sugar stay with me in memory.

12

I write a string of postcards. To Mr Roopratna an elephant adorned for the Pahera at Kandy. I struggle with a strange script and easy phrases, hoping he will understand.

When I return to the Palm Garden I ask about the card, but he only shakes his head sadly as if feeling my disappointment.

Towards the middle of April the monsoon lost patience with the season and made its first afternoon raids along the coast, as if some marauding pirate intent on riches. The rain fell heavy and straight out of a jungle-black sky. More leaves fell into the Palm Garden. Mr Roopratna was slower in their retrieval and spent more time listening to the radio in the early evenings. I filled the spaces with long, fat, meaningless books and tried to ignore a chorus of frogs that sang enthusiastically, welcoming the rain.

Celebrations to usher the start of the new year were beginning in the village, marked by a procession of pilgrims and a bicycle race. Fireworks escaped early from their dry calm, scattering sparks and thunderclaps throughout the houses beneath the trees.

Mr Roopratna appeared to wither as the celebrations gained momentum, and a day before the official New Year he was waiting for me on the verandah with a crumpled newspaper.

He pointed to the script, which I couldn't understand,

13

but there was a blurred photograph tacked onto the front page. It looked like a ship lying forlorn on its side in shallow water, its hull and purpose holed at the waterline; dark scars of a fierce fire marked the metal.

'Trinco?'

He nodded sadly.

'Your sons?'

His head dropped as he mumbled to himself before retreating to the rear of the bungalow.

The world service gave the barest of details. A suicide attack on a gunship at Trincomalee. The Tamil Tigers had claimed responsibility. There were seventeen dead. Another quick, brutal tragedy was carried briefly before they moved onto another, the execution of a housemaid in Singapore.

The morning of the New Year I climbed the hill to the village in the jungle. I was still being paid for a mural in kindness and invites. I clutched a box of biscuits as a gift for the family. The meal arrived in a burst of smiles and small dishes of brinjal and fish curry. I settled back to eat, and the family settled back to watch me.

They kept pointing to my mural on the wall. A bright, easy leopard which snarled out at the children who pretended to be frightened when they played hide and seek with their hands. A couple of neighbours shuffled in to see the visitor eating, armed with shy requests for work.

When I climbed back down to the Palm Garden to the final crescendo of daylight fireworks, De Silva was waiting with a rickshaw, another daughter and an invite.

'You will come for the feast.'

'Now ?'

'Yes, big feast this afternoon.'

The rickshaw moved quickly on the strangely empty roads. People had retreated home for the holiday. De Silva's daughter talked excitedly to her father.

'She asks about the gardener. She likes him.'

'His sons?'

'Yes, his sons. They came to collect him this morning.'

'I thought they were in Trinco? The bombing?'

'No, no, they're on leave. They came to take him back to his wife for the New Year.'

'His wife?' The flow of words accelerated beyond the rickshaw as my fixed imagination refocused hazily.

'Yes, he has a wife and daughters, Badulla side. He goes to visit them every two months or so.'

The girl at his side added another question, which he answered but didn't translate.

A week passes after the New Year. I begin again on my canvasses, but the garden seems very quiet without Mr Roopratna. The visiting monkeys are miserable and silent, subdued by the rain and distrusting of the slippery branches, now such treacherous friends. The

15

monsoon has filled the wells higher in the village and even the children stay away. Only the roller remains a constant, colouring the mornings.

I buy pineapples from the village and drink arrack in the nights while I plan a flight back, listening to the reports of an escalating war in the North.

I had bought a big bar of chocolate for Mr Roopratna, which waited for him in the fridge. When De Silva arrives for his final month's rent I ask him to make sure the old man receives the gift.

De Silva smiles sadly.

'I'm sorry, I can't. He died a week ago.'

'Died?'

'Hospital. They took him in, not come out.'

'What of ?'

De Silva shrugs his shoulders.

'You come back next year?'

The Fare

Naz had been waiting. The clock clicked forward, timing the day, his fare. Rain traced lines between the droplets on the windscreen, tugging each one down. The wipers swept forward, then back. He checked his watch; the fare was for four-thirty. He wanted to finish by six. He was hungry. He hadn't eaten for nine hours. He didn't like getting up before it was light to eat. It didn't suit him. The days were longer with no food.

He hoped the boy would eat tonight. It had been nine days now. He could see the heat inside his son as it rose to his skin in sweat. But his eyes were still quiet, looking beyond them to somewhere else. The hospital was clean, white and efficient, and it frightened him. The single room surrounded them, hushed.

He needed to finish. Time to eat. Time to visit.

He turned the engine on. A light in the hallway of the house caught him before he could drive the car away. Then the door opened and a man ran from the doorway down the path to the waiting cab.

A rush of cold air filled the car as the man clambered into the back seat. He was out of breath, his coat ruffled up. Naz watched the man as he tried to settle himself and his briefcase into the seat. The man took off his glasses to wipe the steam and rain from the lenses. He peered into the front, up at the mirror, his eyes squinting with the effort.

'Crickhowell House.'

The man spoke with an accent that Naz found difficult.

'Sorry, say again.'

'The Assembly building.'

'Ah, no problem. The bay, yes.'

The man just nodded and turned to face away from the mirror.

Naz concentrated on the traffic ahead as he pulled wide into Cathedral Road. The cars were lined tight, nudging each other out of the city for the weekend. This was a city that dozed through the evenings, only coming awake for a brief few hours between eleven and three, alcohol lowering its inhibitions. It pulled tight to itself during the day. The churches still blistered the city, still calling to it through empty pews. There wasn't enough here yet to break with its past.

Naz had lived in Manchester. It was a real city, full of people, full of the swirl of imagination. There were secret places in that city. Even for him, there were places to drink, to meet women. It was okay to pay for it then. He was a single man. There were necessities he couldn't ignore. He could remember his male friends on the streets at home, holding hands. Frustration dripping between them and not a woman in sight. Death and marriage had saved him from that.

His father had always expected him to give in and come home. The old man was still expecting his son's defeat when he cut into his leg with a cleaver. An accident but still death. Naz had looked for the memory, searched through its corners, even though it couldn't be his. The street thick with the smell of meat. The gutters running with rats and the crows ready to pick scraps from the bones. The panic for a taxi. The blood pouring from the severed artery as his father had seen it pour from so many dying animals, knowing he was dying. Naz had escaped that. His father had died in a taxi on the way to hospital.

The youngest son, he was allowed a chance, a chance to become himself. His brothers had paid for a marriage then. Sure he wasn't coming back. Insuring against him coming back. A proper respectable girl. A good name. Her family lived in Cardiff. They were cousins of a cousin. He would have to move from Manchester. Too many memories, connections for a man about to marry. It was another city, a smaller city.

There were fewer cars going back into the city. It was a straight run, Cathedral Road, Riverside, Grangetown, Butetown, Docks. He could see the faces and houses change colour as he followed the river to the sea.

The man in the back shuffled the papers in his briefcase. He caught Naz looking at him in the mirror and smiled unsurely back.

'I'm late.'

Naz smiled. 'Can't go any faster. The traffic.'

'No, don't suppose you can.' He looked forlorn.

'Important meeting?'

The man looked as if he didn't quite understand the question.

'At the Assembly?' prompted Naz.

'No, not really. A commission.'

'You're an important man?'

The man straightened himself in the back seat. He looked to see if Naz was mocking him. It was a straight question.

'Er, no, I don't suppose I am.'

'What's the rush then?'

The man looked away. He watched the river rush below him and the space where there had once been factories now filled with cleared land. A sign marked the opportunit: 'Open to offers!'

The radio crackled through. Naz picked it up. A voice told him he had another call at the university. He could go home then. Narine would be waiting for him. She had been at the hospital for days. They allowed her to sleep there at first. Waiting. But she couldn't sleep and she just spent the nights staring out across the lights that marked the limits of the city. Naz liked the view from the ward. It was the only thing he liked about the hospital. At nights he could see the towns on the far side of the estuary and imagine what it would be like living there. Anywhere but here, now, while his dreams struggled through in the bed beneath him. It was a strange country, this. A country trying to find its way. There was nothing he could see that wasn't just smaller than Manchester.

He had taken Narine, the boy and the baby out to the coast last summer. The little boy had played in the waves as if they were something new and unique, especially provided for him. Narine had prepared dahl and chappattis which they ate on a rug placed over the sand. He could feel the stares; unease or novelty, he couldn't be sure. He tried to ignore them. The beach was packed with children, kites, dogs, sandcastles, the debris of a day out. Naz had been filled with the wealth of summer, the God-willing luck that had provided him with a wife and child. Narine couldn't swim, but she went into the water in her suit. The boy had played with the ball, and the waves had played with him. It had been a good day. He would be a father again in the spring, but that was a long way back through the winter now.

The traffic lights held him on the corner of Bute and James Street. An ambulance streaked past. Blue lights flooding the cab. The man in the back leaned over to get a better look at the road.

'I didn't think it was going to be like this?'

Naz looked up at the mirror to see the man's face. Lines of stress seemed to have cut into him.

'It's the time of night.'

'No, not the traffic. The city, this country. I don't understand it.'

The lights allowed the car to move forward. Naz checked his watch.

'What time is your meeting?'

'It doesn't matter.'

The man seemed to collapse back into himself.

'It is your country?'

'Yes, but I can't escape from it.' The man struggled in his pockets for money.

The edifice of the Assembly building rose out of the rain. It was spotlighted but seemed unsure of itself on the stage in this new half-country.

Naz pulled the car into a lay-by opposite the building. Four pounds forty was displayed on the clock. The man handed him a five pound note. Naz knew he would require change.

'Can I have a receipt, please?'

Naz scribbled the amount on the back of a card. His writing had never been as good as his speech, but he was okay on the numbers. The man pocketed his change and the receipt. He got out of the cab and shut the door. Naz pulled the car back onto the road and headed into town.

He didn't like calls at the university. They were usually students. There were too many students in the city. The city swelled with them every October, gorging itself on their easy money. But by December he was tired of their jokes, their endless enthusiasm and the way they threw up in his car. Today was the last day of term. He kept up with these events. He used them to

24

mark his time in the city. Six years now. Six years with a new wife and now two children. The first one was a boy, that was good. The next a girl. That was good also but maybe more expensive. Still he loved girls and the way she opened her eyes to him. He would earn enough money. He would be successful in this city. His father-in-law had offered to lend him some money to start a business. It was good to be in business. In business for yourself. He knew about the cars. There would be younger men keen to work longer hours as the city expanded. He wouldn't be a younger man much longer. Then he would need to make a business.

The car pushed itself along the flyover that cut back into the centre of the city. The road rose steeply, soaring above the railway line and the units that lined its route out to the east. From the top the city was all briefly visible before the road crashed into the walls of the prison and the horizon reduced itself to streets again. The traffic slowed him again at the law courts. He wasn't sure if the fare would still be waiting at the university. People called through then forgot about it.

The students reminded him. There had been a ripple of meningitis cases last winter. He had seen their faces in *The Echo*. Bright, young, hopeful, dead. It took them so quickly. A few days of coughs and headaches and then a sharp coma. There had been a man working in a restaurant he had heard about, a

25

Hindu. He was working on Monday night, in hospital by Tuesday. He had only lasted two days. There was a picture of him behind the counter in the restaurant. A big smiling man. The boy was a fighter. A strong boy. He could feel the determination in his arms as he clambered around his shoulders, mouthing words in two languages. It had been too many days, the dark days of winter in the city. He called back into the radio. He was signing off for the night. There was a brief complaint from the operator on the far side of the call. Then he put the handset down.

A month ago he had followed the cars to the cemetery. They had been given a plot out in Ely, a few miles to the west of the city. The graves were new. They had been cut deeply into the soft Welsh loam. Each new mound, a life ending out here, many miles from the start in a dusty village on the Indus plain, or the crumbling walls of Lahore or Karachi. The cities themselves had changed their names, as if able to disown their children. They couldn't return to a place that no longer existed. They had cut themselves off and would now be the first to die in this new place where it rained through the long winters. He had thought of their hopes. Many of the graves carried pictures of them as young men. Faded, overexposed pictures of dark men in poor new suits, eager for a go at the world. Most had thought they would go back.

They had listened solemnly in the mosque off Crwys Road. The walls dripped with the sounds of his childhood and the cool mornings in Peshawar before the sun got too high. The time to work. His father had been keen on education, avoided politics. The future was commerce.

The new mosque had been a factory, making clothes. They bought it with donations and optimism. He never attended much himself. The community was growing. He could buy Halal meat now and vegetables he hadn't seen since he left Manchester. His wife bought clothes from people who could speak Urdu.

The meat was good but to be avoided in memory of his father. But it was there, fresh and available. They had some strength now, numbers, a community. The boy would be starting school in a year. He would learn English properly then.

There were casualties. His closest friend ran a chip shop in Llanrumney and was living with a woman called Ruth. He had given up the cars. He was too old for the abuse and the girls who wouldn't pay you and the men who simply walked away. He would trust in Allah, he had claimed, and now he was sending money to a woman he had married and living with one he hadn't. But Naz couldn't leave the faith. It was part of him. The inscription above the door convinced him. Allah is good. Allah is great. And indeed he had been. But now, with his son at the hospital, he wasn't so sure. The little boy had committed no sin, but then he remembered his own nights on the riverside in Manchester.

He drove the car along Richmond Road, across the junction. The lights favouring his flight. He pulled up at number forty-seven Mackintosh Place. The lights were on in the front room. He could feel the tension in his fingers as he cut the engine and opened the car door. The door to his house was ajar; he could smell the good smells of cooking flood through him. He found Narine in the kitchen. She was sitting at the table slumped over, her head resting. He touched her hair. She stood up and folded into him. He knew his daughter was being cared for; he knew the boy had gone.

We Were Winning

Lee had only just joined the team. He was a quiet lad. He lived up on the Maes Glas estate with his mother. I sometimes dropped him off on my way home. The boys didn't say much about him. He was in the other school in the centre of town and his Welsh didn't come easily to him so they spoke to him only in English. Or maybe he was just quiet and it was a new area. I think his mother had moved across from Carmarthen last summer. But he could kick a football alright. He really had something. The way he could hold a ball up, feint to shoot, then slide a pass through a set of defenders as if they were stuck to the pitch.

We weren't having the best of starts. A couple of the boys had joined the rugby team instead while a few had just drifted away over the summer, picked up on the computer games. You had to have keen parents to get you up to Y Parc every Saturday for 9 a.m. Lee's mother dropped him off. She didn't stay to talk to any of the other mothers. She just whispered something to him before he climbed out of the car and then drove off. She spoke to me the first time to introduce herself and Lee.

'I rang you about Lee joining? He wants to play where he can score goals.' She wore a waterproof jacket that was at least three sizes too big for her. She still had some make-up smeared around her eyes.

'We'll see what we can do then.'

'Would you be able to drop him back for me? I've got to work in Tesco's. He's got a key.'

And that was it. I only gave him a half the first few weeks to let him settle in. I told him to play at the back. We didn't concede many goals when he was playing but we were still losing. The boys wanted to know when I was going to play him up front but you can't rush these things. I had to give him time to adjust.

I made the mistake of asking him if his father was going to come to see him play... *I don't know who my father is...* put me in my place... the way he said it, a challenge – *so what – aren't I good enough for you then?*

I've got used to the breakdown bit; more than half the team are in a process of transition in the domestic area. Catrin reckons it's the Internet. Not sure what the hell that has got to do with it. Maybe she knows more than me though – working at the Post Office you get to know a lot about people, maybe too much – she's had enough of it. I look at computers for a living, last thing I want to do when I get back is get on-line and talk to some long-lost girlfriend.

I first clocked the old guy about a month after Lee had started. He was standing up on the halfway line under a big red umbrella, which was a bit odd as it wasn't raining. You get to know the parents who turn up to support so I just assumed he was one of the Drefach lot. They like their umbrellas up there. They hadn't brought enough players for a full team so I had to lend them two of ours. I gave them Rhydian because he couldn't kick a ball if it bit him and Lee.

32

That was a mistake. I could see it in his eyes when I asked him to play for them that maybe it wasn't such a good idea. The boys whispered to me, 'What you do that for Mr Arnold?' Maybe my team management skills need a bit of improving.

Lee scored the first goal straight from the kick-off. Drefach lobbed a long ball to no one in particular and Lee chased it, caught it in front of our defence, turned and hit it in from twenty yards. Our goalkeeper hadn't even put his gloves on. It was the first of five. Every time he scored the man under the red umbrella seemed to jump up and down in excitement.

As our team trudged off on the end of a six-one hammering, the man with the red umbrella walked across the pitch towards the boys. He was waving at Lee. Lee saw him coming and began running away. The man started running after him. I was running now as well; something wasn't quite right. Lee was too quick anyway and the man stopped. He was breathing heavily when I got to him and there were tears in his eyes.

'Are you alright mate?'

He looked up at me and wiped his eyes with his jumper.

'Yes, I'm fine... give him this will you.'

He passed a crumpled five pound note to me and then walked away.

By the time I caught up with Lee and the other boys

I could see he'd been crying as well. I thought I'd better ignore it. But he spoke on the way back in the car.

'That was my grandfather. Mam says I shouldn't speak to him. What do you think Mr Arnold?'

What the hell was I supposed to say? I've done my coaching badges – but they didn't ask me that one on the half-day at Aberystwyth leisure centre. Rhydian and Carl sniggered in the back, and I told them to shut up – they listened to that. I dropped Lee off at his house. Two of the windows had been boarded up at the front. The boys looked at the house in disbelief. After Lee got out they were still looking at the boarded frames.

'What happened to the windows Mr Arnold?'

I made sure he was playing the next week. The boys insisted, but even I could see talent by that point. I had been hoping he would develop into an effective right-back. A right-back that could score five goals in a game? We started to win straight away. Lee was able to control a match. He wasn't any bigger than anyone else, but he wanted the ball, and when he kicked it he knew where it was going.

There was no league as such, just a succession of friendlies, but the news of Lee's scoring potential soon got around. Someone even said there was a scout from the Swans at one of the games. I didn't see him though. His grandfather was at all the games, always on the halfway line, always with a red umbrella. I could see

34

that Lee looked for him when they ran out on the pitch. He didn't shout encouragement, but he jumped around whenever Lee scored, as if the effort of remaining composed were too much for him. After a few weeks Lee would walk over to him at the end of the game and they would talk. Just a few words and just long enough for the grandfather to give his grandson five pounds. It saved him having to give it to me to give it to him. Lee always looked a bit guilty when he returned late to the changing huddle but the other boys didn't seem to notice. He was too much one of them by then.

The year moved on quickly. My work wasn't going too well. They offered voluntary redundancy to a few in my department. I was tempted. Catrin wanted a new challenge away from the Post Office. I didn't really want to move. Christmas came and went. I saw Lee's mother in a pub in town. She was with a couple of girls on a night out. She was wearing a Christmas hat with mistletoe dangling in front of it. I was with a few of the lads from the golf club. I got home at three in the morning.

Just before Easter we entered the County five-a-side tournament in Aber. Lee was the star from the start. There were fewer objects to get in his way, and we cruised through the rounds. Lee had scored eleven goals by the final, and there was quite a crowd watching him. The final was against the home team. They were much bigger than us. I'm still sure a few of their boys were overage. They'd obviously been watching us play as well because they went for Lee from the start. They must have been told to kick him. I was shouting at the ref; their supporters were shouting at me. He got up the first time and got on with it – the second time he stayed down. He looked hurt. I got on with the water and the magic sponge.

'That wasn't fair Mr Arnold – they just kicked me.'

I splashed water on his shins. A bruise was rushing to the surface of his skin, colouring red. Lee's grandfather came across.

'Are you alright son?'

'Yes Da. I'm fine.'

'Good, get up then, you've got a game to win.'

'I will Da.'

Lee got up shakily; his leg was cut but he ran back into the game.

I suppose it was fortunate the next pass went to Carl. Aber were used to kicking by that point, so they just kicked him as well. Carl wasn't going to be kicked by anyone, so he just got up and lashed out at the nearest player. It was uproar. These parents are bloody terrible when they get too involved – shouting, swearing, threatening the referee. The referee called the whole thing off. It was all over the *Cambrian News*. Under 11 Five-A-Side Football Tournament Abandoned For Crowd Trouble. Bloody hell mun, we were winning. I had to appear before the County Football Association.

I thought I was going to lose my badges, but they just banned the other coach and gave me a reprimand.

Lee's grandfather was waiting for me after I'd changed. I introduced myself as we shook hands.

'James Arnold...'

'Wyn Rees... quite a team you have there.'

'I'm not sure about a team. Lee scores the goals.'

'There's a few tidy players as well as our boy. Is he alright?'

'Yeh, I think so. You're his granddad?'

'Yes, don't get to see him much, not since his mum and dad split – we don't get to see him – my wife doesn't get about much now – she's over there in the car. Do you think we could take him out for supper?'

'I can't do that Mr Rhys. I've got to get him back home. Couldn't you ask his mother?'

'Sian won't speak to us. It's hard you know, we're missing him, missing him growing up. Could you ask him to come over to say hello to his grandma though?'

I went back into the clubhouse. The adults were standing around talking, trying to forget how embarrassing they'd been twenty minutes earlier. The boys were all eating crisps and drinking orange squash provided by the club. The heat of the game was gone. The boys were still little boys. Lee was talking to Carl, and Rhydian was pointing at something in his hand and laughing. Just small boys.

I called Lee over – told him his grandfather and

nanna wanted to speak to him. He looked up at me for an answer.

'It won't hurt. I'll come with you.'

We walked across the car park to where his grandfather was waiting by the side of his car. His grandmother had got out. She was sitting in a wheelchair. I watched as Lee walked across to them and then bent down to kiss her.

The season finished soon after that. The summer passed quickly as they always do. When the new season started most of the boys came back, but there was no sign of Lee. I called up to his house on Maes Glas. The window had been repaired, but there was an old man with a dog living there. He didn't know where they had gone. *I should ask the social maybe.* I heard a few weeks later that Lee's mother had a new boyfriend and moved in with him. I think they were living over towards Carmarthen. I hope Lee's playing football.

An Immediate Man

James Willis does not consider himself an immediate man. For a man in love with the present this is a major problem.

Willis is buying books on the Charing Cross Road. She is glancing out at him from Grade's. Secure in a black-and-white still. He knows the face from a time of Saturday afternoons when there was nothing else but a visit to the cinema. His father smiling and happy in drink as he waits for them to emerge. She looks shyly into the camera, a half glance, conscious it does not always treat her kindly. But when it does. Her name hesitates in his mind, something foreign, perhaps French but probably further East. It will not come. A score of films or maybe only two. He names a handful of possible co-stars she may have kissed. There is a bubble of feeling. Willis smiles, enters Grade's and buys the print.

He discovers her name is Jane Davilre. His research is thorough. She surfaces in London as part of the flotsam of the European war. Ja changes to Jane in a name that always makes the credits on the big screen. Twenty or thirty films follow each other effortlessly before she fades as quickly as she appeared into the anonymity of the city.

Willis begins to collect stills of her; they are rare but collectable. He is seen regularly on the Portobello Road. He has bought six when he sees her move again. Her name calls out to him as he scans the week's listings.

41

It still has cachet for the present editors. The sound has resonance of romance and rationing that is irresistible.

It is showing at one of those cinemas on Marsden Road that feed the city's insatiable appetite for nostalgia on a Wednesday afternoon. Its ageless streets a constant cradle and grave, of a certain age and memory.

Willis waits expectantly before the vacant screen. The cinema is warm but empty. The scattered patrons try with some difficulty not to attract each other's attention before the lights dim discreetly.

She plays a widowed French aristocrat who hides an injured British fighter pilot in a narrow Brittany fishing village. There is much footage of cliff tops in Cornwall, rough seas and Gestapo staff cars. The plot follows her love affair with the airman as she nurses him back to health. The conflict revolves around the unwelcome amorous attentions of a handsome but obviously evil German officer. The twist, because there is always a twist, when she seduces the German allowing the hero to escape onto a waiting fishing smack.

Willis absorbs the film. Her face impossibly large in the fullness of the screen. He experiences a curious sense of jealousy as she kisses the airman which turns to lust as she seduces the officer.

The journey home is painful. The scarred German begs for change. The airman asks for his tube ticket.

Back at his flat he rings Laura who does not refuse an invitation for food and sex.

42

The next film is in London. Willis recognises the plane trees full with summer rain sheltering the Regency squares, as she runs from cab to doorway. The unfaithful wife of an American ambassador bribed into revealing military secrets. Willis is the dark Russian with the heavy accent. It makes BBC 2 on a Sunday afternoon. Laura is not available, so he pays for a prostitute. He tapes the film for rehearsal and notes.

The prints replace original oils on the walls of his flat. Harry, genial and horrible, calls them gauche and sneers. Willis barely resists the temptation to break his nose.

He spends a week in the British Library reading newspapers, which culminates in a letter to Westminster Council requesting a blue plaque for a guest house in Bartley Road. There is no reply.

Laura, naked and laughing, teases him about the new woman he's neglecting her for. Willis, not teasing, begins to strangle her in the sex that follows. She forces him off, fear in her eyes.

The letter is a chance. Her name, beloved of casting directors, has remained in the directory. Still deliberately isolated. Cadogan Place is only a few minutes away by cab, but he writes the letter. The best affairs are begun in ink. He allows the roll of corrupted French to caress his tongue before he seals the envelope.

The reply is carefully charming. Ms Davilre would be pleased to meet Mr James Willis to discuss art, literature and everything. Her lips from a Cornish cliff top return immediately to his imagination. There is a trip to Paris and a room booked in Montparnasse. He keeps the receipts.

Willis arrives early at the Regency Rooms. An odd choice he considers. He imagines somewhere more provocative. The tables are deserted except for a delicate couple obviously from the provinces and an old lady crowned by a purple hat with silver brocade.

He waits in silence, casually checking his watch between gentle sips from a glass of house red. He expects her to be late. There is no style for a woman in being early.

Ten minutes drift carelessly into twenty then thirty. The couple from the provinces leaves, and an aproned waitress appears to clear away the plates. The old woman smiles at him. He half smiles out of habit as he turns away, wishing old women wouldn't make themselves faintly ridiculous by trying to be young. He checks his watch again, irritably. It is the right teahouse, he's sure of that. The Regency Rooms on the lake. He reaches for the letter in his suit pocket when his hand stops and returns to the wine.

He turns uneasily to look at the last remaining customer. Her smile is unsure but hopeful. His stare returns quickly to the lake beyond the windows.

Willis fumbles without success for change in his wallet. He leaves a five pound note on the napkin close to the empty glass. A residue of red transparent in its

44

well. Not looking at anyone except a still memory on Charing Cross Road, he walks out of the tea room into the languid park that is again summer in ageless charm.

Dave Tillers

Dave Tillers has been my name for fifteen years. A poor name I've thought, uneven. I always considered David would have sounded more complete. But it seemed to thrive; growing; aging as it assumed me.

The pilot had been costed for a nine-week trial. Pitched as a tough Black Country drama by a new independent outfit, it was to be focused on 'real people, real stories.'

Chance suggested it would broaden my appeal. A positive diversion from the run of interesting but average parts I'd been picking up on the stage. Policemen with a past, tormented priests, old soldiers. All drifting in the background of the main action. I was there for substance; depth to the brittle scripts which never threatened to move me forward. I was the character man throwing a couple of brutal lines into the mix as the story drifted towards the second act.

Dave Tillers was another man with a past. A garage owner nudging forty with a teenage daughter at the local comp but no visible wife. I was in for the substance again. Chance was convinced it would raise my stage fees. He was right about that.

'A TV number, easy money. Six weeks of filming, starts on the eighth. No need to audition, the casting director saw you as Williams at the York.'

I enjoyed the filming. Everyone clowning around on a big budget and the money was good. Paid for a holiday to Morocco and a second-hand Volvo.

The pilot series went out in the summer. An hour-long primer followed by eight half-hour slots. The production company were obviously hoping for big figures and they got them. Peaking at nine million on a Tuesday evening in the third week of August. People must have forgotten to go on holiday this year. The station was euphoric; the next run was booked for the spring. Advertisers were pushing for a weekly slot. The story appealed to the viewers they were targeting: people running the nine-to-five with money to spend at the weekends.

Tillers' Garage got a big audience-recognition figure, and the role was raised for the second run. Planned as a weekly for six months, I'm still in it.

The nation followed Dave as I lurched from one failed romance to another. My daughter became pregnant, married and moved south. I still see her in the occasional bit part in one of the detective dramas. Her husband's got a property business, and she has a couple of children. I employed a succession of lads on the various government training schemes; they all moved on. None of them really made it. The business prospered and expanded, then faltered to the verge of bankruptcy before recovering on the insurance payout from a suspicious fire that proved to be accidental. I was robbed twice, once at gunpoint, then found myself facing two years on a GBH charge after stopping a third robbery with the rough end of a monkey wrench.

My wife appeared for a stretch, a sharp fiery woman

from Cork. I juggled two affairs for a torrid six months before losing them both.

I began being recognised almost immediately. It was a bit scary at first: strangers smiling, kids shouting 'Tillers' across a crowded street on a Saturday morning. You try to ignore it, but sometimes people are more direct and sometimes it's nice. I was asked for a job on a Friday night at The Unicorn. The man was thirty-two, had served his apprenticeship with a further ten years experience, five as a fitter in the Signals. He offered me references.

Of course the stage roles improved. Chance had been right on that one. A score of well-received pieces before I began to decline the offers. I'm not sure why; perhaps it was the time, but the money seemed paltry. The Christmas shows were more lucrative and the lines hardly mattered. I could improvise and the kids still laughed. My name was three feet high below a professionally backlit stage photograph, but everyone was there to see Tillers play the ugly sister.

Towards the end of the ninth year I negotiated for a break. The producers assumed I was after more money and called my hand. Unfortunately for them I played through. My public reacted savagely. Tillers' exit was blamed on everything from alcoholism to the decline of the Midlands manufacturing industry. The papers ran polls confidently predicting the demise of the show.

The producers swallowed hard, ordered a mid-life

crisis, a long month's holiday and doubled my money.

The drinking began a year later. It started as a joke during a Christmas party at The George. I sailed through a bottle of vodka, made a pass at the barmaid, who was younger than my pregnant daughter, before stumbling into a fight with the landlord.

The audience loved it. The nationals carried pictures of me being arrested in the street. Headlines screaming 'Tillers Arrested Again.' I escaped with a caution after the landlord decided not to press charges.

A month or two later I got pulled on a drink-driving charge. A two-year ban blazed across the front pages. I began drinking on set. Not too much, a few bottles of lager a day. It kept the pressure off.

A running argument developed with the chief script editor. He accused me of trying to rewrite the story. So what? I went my own way, and he only lasted another series.

Towards the end of the twelfth year I'd had enough. I made two serious attempts at leaving, but again they increased the money. Eventually they realise they can't afford another offer.

The way I look at it I've got a good ten years left. I could retire, the money's certainly there, but I need to get rid of Tillers. Just for myself.

Chance has picked up a couple of parts for the spring. One's an Edwardian melodrama but the other's a new play, Scottish writer, already picked up a couple of awards. A real play, something to do with the New Russia. A co-production of politics and vodka. Smirnoff and the Scottish Arts Council are sponsoring it. It'll be a good season.

Need to finish the final two months. I think they've written a garage accident, trying to make a point about safety at work. Tillers is looking a bit run-down these days. There's rumours that he's been hitting the bottle.

II TAKE 2 THE AGENT

I'm not sure how much Brian realised he'd become Tillers. He was Tillers, still is.

I picked the role for him in the first place. The casting director owed me a favour. I could see it was going to run. Brian needed it, a succession of dead-end supporting roles and he was going nowhere. He'd have been washed up in another five years. He was drinking too much back then. But the role suited him. He even acted it off the set, the drinking, the women, the brawls. Always a bit of a lad. But it was good publicity. He made a fortune every Christmas in those awful pantomimes I pushed his way. By then getting him money was the least of my worries. One producer wanted an assurance he wouldn't forget his lines. For Christ sake it was only a pantomime. I told him it was Dave Tillers he was booking. He won't need to know any lines. Anyway he was good at improvisation, pissed or not.

53

Of course he's tried to leave before. First time he even had me fooled. I really thought he wanted out. Told the producers he was going, couldn't talk him out of it. Christ even I believed him. Then the publicity hit and they doubled the money. Doubled it. He was making a fortune anyway. This is prime time. He fooled us that time alright; sometimes I think he's a better actor than we give him credit for. This time, though, he's had it. They've written him out. A heavy drinking session too many, turns into work still pissed and slam, a Volvo comes down on top of him. What a way to go for the nation's favourite mechanic. He didn't seem to mind when I told him. Guess he's got all philosophical about it. He's fifty-five, time to get out. He's certainly got enough money to retire and he's more or less paid for mine as well. Claims he wants a couple of stage roles again. Must be crazy, wanting to get back in front of an audience; should have seen some of his set performances the last few years. Twenty-eight takes, one of them. He already held the show record. But his name carries money now, so I got him a couple for the spring season. Nothing too demanding, an uncle in some period farce the Rep are knocking out for the retired set and a bit part in a new play by that Scottish writer. The director was a bit dubious, but the writer used to watch Tillers as a kid and is keen to have him in. Might even pick up a good review for that one, if he can stay together. It's only thirty lines.

TAKE 3 DIRECTOR, WRITER, PRODUCER

'Look, I don't care, we just can't do it.'

'Why not?'

'It's not decent, this is still a family show.'

'Oh c'mon.'

'We go out before nine. If you still hadn't noticed?'

'Yeh and what about Simon and Gary? They're a nice respectable couple.'

'That story line has nothing to do with it, it's very tactfully done, it confronts the issues and deals with them.'

'Bollocks. It's sensationalist crap. A furtive kiss outside the pub before Christmas, holding hands on the settee.'

'Can we get away from Simon and Gary please? They're fictional and this, if I can remind you both, is not.'

'Dave Tillers has been a real person for fifteen years. Remember the drink-driving charge and the affairs. He is Dave Tillers. This is real, a real end to Tillers.'

'I'm sorry, it's too real for me.'

'Rubbish. Look at Monday's papers. They're thick with the show, front page again. You can't buy this much publicity. I say we screen it a week today.'

'Well?'

'Never, it's disgusting. He's still trying to write one of his fucking brutal screen one's they're always rejecting.'

'Fuck you.'

'This is getting us nowhere. We'll see the edit again.'

'I don't believe this.'

The producer pressed the video control. The writer and director watched. The picture flashed to focus as the lights in the room automatically dimmed.

Dave Tillers is standing on his garage forecourt looking into the engine of a shining blue Astra.

'Yeh, spin her.'

The engine grates to a stirring rattle, but there is no progression to the smooth, comforting sound of a functioning machine.

'Again.'

The procedure is repeated for the same result.

'Right, Spike, the starting motor's had it. Get onto Joe's to see if he's got one off the shelf. If not order it.'

Spike emerges from the driver's seat and peers intently into the engine.

'Not there, here. The motor's here. What are they teaching you on that one-day-a-week in tech? Ay? How to talk to women? Not much use in a garage I can tell you.'

'I told you I'm doing the public relations course.'

Spike looks up enough to see Dave Tillers beginning to sway, then fall back, grasping at the sides of the car before crashing to the floor. The panic on Spike's face is real.

The producer cuts to the pause button as people rush

in from the sides of the set. The lights come up in the room. The writer is first to speak.

'There we've got two seconds clear, cut there and run the credits. It's too good to pass up.'

'Christ, the man's in fucking hospital.'

'Did you see the look on Spike's face? They don't teach you that in drama school. Best two seconds of acting he's ever put in.'

'Christ.'

'I can see what you're getting at, but the man's in hospital?'

'Don't you think I know that? I've spoken to the consultant today.'

'And?'

'He's conscious.'

'So?'

'Chance reckons he'll go for it.'

'You've put it to his agent?'

'Someone had to do it.'

'You're all feeling.'

'It's not such a problem. He wanted out anyway, a month early is no problem. We've already put in the buildup. He's been on the vodka heavy for three weeks, he's just had the news about his daughter. The public are waiting for it. They know he's had a haemorrhage. They want to see it.'

The writer looks at the producer. This is the moment.

'Get him to sign a disclaimer.'

Jeffrey Chance sat on on the side of the bed clutching his briefcase close to his bulging stomach. A briefcase with a final contract for forty thousand pounds. The conversation was proving more difficult than he had expected. Much more difficult than he had expected. He could feel the sweat beginning to form on the back of his neck.

'Yes of course, Mr Chance, I'll be back, no problem.'

There was an edge to Brian's voice that unnerved Chance. A deep-seated, thick, Black Country edge. He recalled a fraught conversation with Helen, Brian and Dave's latest affair. She was a sweet young actress working in the café.

'He's confused, Mr Chance. He's not remembering things clearly.' Her voice cracking into tears on the telephone.

'There's no problem with the garage.' Brian was talking but the words were slipping over Chance. 'Spike can keep it ticking over for a week or two if you could just supervise the finance side of it. Twenty percent as usual.'

'Yes, but Brian.'

Dave Tillers looked up uncertainly from the depths of his white bed before Chance realised his mistake.

'Dave, you're due to be written out? You've signed, agreed retirement.'

'Leave the garage? I don't know what you're on about Mr Chance? We just had two new contracts through. I just need a couple more days and I'll be back.'

'Yes, I know, but in the spring, the new Scottish play?' Chance struggled to find a way forward.

'No, only a week. Spike can manage till then.'

Chance looked out across the city from Brian's private room. Dave Tillers coughed, waiting. Chance turned to face him.

'Perhaps if you can just sign these documents for me then?'

'What are they ?'

'Financial formalities.'

'Sure, Mr Chance, always leave the accounts to you.'

Chance shuffled the documents towards Dave Tillers who struggled to scrawl his strange, unfamiliar signature.

Feeding the House Crows

I shouted hard, trying to deflect the man's threat, but he just smiled, motioned with his arms over brown spindle legs and thin stretched ribs before extending his open palm to me once again. I closed my eyes, lay back against my heavy green rucksack and imagined myself on a beach in the south.

A thin, bearded Norwegian at a rest house in Hardwar had told me it was bad karma to ignore the requests of a sadhu. We had been drinking tea on the terrace in the early morning, warm and comfortable before the real heat of the day. A man had appeared at our table. He was naked except for a deeply stained orange loincloth that was curled around his waist and draped over his right shoulder. The solitary waiter noticed his presence but refrained from approaching. He didn't say anything, just offered his hand, calloused and empty, which the Norwegian filled with a roll of brown notes. The hand moved in my direction, and I complied without thinking. His eyes registered no reaction as he spirited the money into a fold concealed within his cloth.

My companion seemed unconcerned by the trans-action, but I couldn't shake the feeling I'd been rifled. The eyes had given nothing to me. Just a calm acceptance of my money. I was just drifting past. Someone not from his world. Empty.

The beggar, dressed in the same orange cloth of a holy man, must have followed me through the tight throng of travellers on the station platform. I had secured a square of empty floor space on the far side of the rest rooms. The train was delayed, and it was late into the long, tense afternoons that stretch through the winter on the Ganges plain. He appeared as I turned to check the clock.

A mass of black matted hair that merged with a thick, betel-stained beard. Faint smells of sandalwood and sweat. Three teeth surfaced from behind the hair as his first request for alms was refused.

Initially I tried to look beyond him, concentrate on the peopled platform that grew and surged in anticipation of the expected train still a hundred miles away. A single house crow skipped down between the oily rails, searching for the scraps of dried paratha an old woman had thrown away from her meal. It dug quickly twice under a sleeper before lifting sharply upwards to a beam across the arched roof.

The sadhu didn't move, just waited. I looked directly at him, waved a hand firmly and shook my head.

His teeth slid away, but his eyes still held me, and a hand remained outstretched.

I shrugged before brushing the dust on the floor clear for a seat. The man squatted where he was. The hand still asking.

I took a book from the side pocket of the rucksack and pretended to read, but my concentration held only in short bursts punctuated by the continued insistence of the man's presence that I should give him money.

'No, not today.'

The shout had no effect on him but succeeded in attracting the attention of a trio of suited businessmen who were playing a game of standing cards a short distance down the platform. I watched as they discussed the odd duo facing each other. The sadhu had marked me out. He had approached no one else and now squatted obstinately a yard away, palm out-stretched, impassively open, waiting for my reaction.

Other heads turned as the continuous traffic of people coursed up and down the platform. A girl with big brown bug eyes pointed; her mother followed her gaze before sharply pulling her away.

'Why not ask somebody else?' I gestured. A few interested heads turned back but the sadhu was fixed. They were of his religion, I assumed, but I had money. It would only take a handful of rupees, but I couldn't force myself to open the money belt that stuck with sweat and dust to my waist.

The man pulled his cloth further from his body to emphasise the fact that he had nothing. Desired nothing. Nothing permanent. The money would only buy him food.

One of his testicles hung forward from the side of his loincloth, long black hairs pulling the skin to small nodules on his scrotum. It lolled in the open before he eased it back with a push of his finger.

I shifted uneasily against my rucksack. An announcement strained through the public address

65

system. A baby cried before being pushed inside its mother's sari. Shyly the woman pulled a hood over her head to protect them.

The voice was consumed by the shimmering heat that festered under the ochre-shaded beams of the station roof. People stirred, shifted, checked possessions and children, but there was no movement to the edge.

'Go away.' I emphasised each syllable.

One of the businessmen who had been playing a hand of cards tapped the squatting sadhu lightly on the shoulder. He didn't look up. The action was repeated with the same result.

There was an unease as the businessman touched the sadhu's shoulder. He was reluctant to directly confront him. It was a request for attention, and it was being denied.

He cautiously suggested a question. It was a polite petition, a reasoning that I sensed, even though I understood nothing of the rising flowing words. The sadhu waved his hand away brusquely. The man looked at me, shrugged his shoulders and returned to his friends. They waited for the next development.

I turned my head down. I could wait until the train arrived. Then it was sixteen hours on a sleeper. Tomorrow would be another city, another place, and this station would be a memory to store with the rush of people and places that was becoming India.

More time slithered by. Seconds moving on. Waiting.

The only thing the man carried was a leather pouch strung by hide around his neck to his waist. As he demanded with one hand, the other would gently ease up and touch the bag as if to ascertain that the charm was still there.

Now he clasped this bag tightly and began murmuring something low and unintelligible.

'English mate, speak English,' I shouted at him. I could sense a sap of anger rising but a public show of aggression would get me nowhere. This was a holy man. Everyone showed deference.

His murmuring continued, deep, guttural sounds uttered without moving his lips. He loosened the string that clasped the leather pouch together and pulled out what I first thought were white incense sticks. But as he opened his hand he revealed a necklace of small bones strung together on a string of gut. Three bones tangled together, they looked like femurs, but tiny, delicate femurs six inches long. He lifted them to his mouth, pursed his lips gently over their bleached surface before allowing two to fall from his hand, holding the gut between his forefinger and thumb. They bounced, then swayed as he drew small circular motions in the air.

I woke to a rush of steam, noise and adrenaline that floods into a platform with a late train. Panic screamed through me as I reached for the rucksack, but it was there, green and comforting, with its bulk and promise of useful possessions. The moving crowd surged around, the beggar gone.

The scramble for the train continued unabated. The long wait had sharpened everyone's need to be away from the city. Stations are designed to be passed through; quickly, without effort. When the flow is baffled, frustrations merge in eddys of stress twisting between the pillars, sharpening tempers, scattering the sparrows that scavenge at the margins.

But the train had arrived. A vast iron carriage in dull amber green, sprayed with the baked brown dust of the Ganges. Figures streamed into open doors, pulling belongings and children through with them. I checked my ticket; it had a number and reservation. But then so did everyone else.

The inside of the carriage bulges and strains as the monster swallows its captives: women with children, men in suits carrying briefcases, an old man twisted with arthritis helped to his seat by a girl.

I secure my seat a third of the way along the carriage. The enthusiasm of the first assault has faded to a determined securing of positions. The number I have drawn is a window berth running parallel to the length of the train and facing a cubicle of six berths at a right angle. The berths are already filled. Bright smiling faces nod in my direction.

I try a simple greeting in Hindi which produces a

duplicate and smiles but no conversation. They probably guess I can't speak it.

The train waits another twenty minutes. The heat in the carriage begins to swarm upward, merging with a thick smell of sweat.

'Chai, chai?' The cry cuts through the carriage as a terracotta bowl of tea is thrust through the open window of my berth. I gladly hand two rupees out to the eager hand.

The tea is warm and sweet, but I feel a shiver of sweat ooze from my skin as I swallow a second time.

The berths opposite are all occupied by men. They seem to be related, as there is a perceptible deference to an older man who dominates the conversation.

I watch as they settle into the compartment. Suitcases are carefully placed on the top bunk; chains appear which are weaved to secure the handles to the steel supports of the sleepers. The middle bunks are folded back to allow the occupants to sit in two rows of three facing each other. They huddle together conspiratorially. I wait for the train to move again.

Then a shiver, a click and the first pull of the engine on the carriage as the machine fights for momentum. There is a subdued cheer as the fixed points on the platform begin to edge past the windows. A warm fetid breeze clamours down through the people; the stagnant air is brushed on.

After the still, listless afternoon the train appears to

move at an incredible speed out of the city. Squat flats decorated with washing and aerials cut into the first thick slums of corrugated iron and plastic festooned with wires and coloured red flags, the sky quartered by dark Pariah Kites. Then a river, peopled and sluggish, with a languorous scum that children splash through. Further out the dwellings thin to tight fields flushed with irrigation channels and watched by egrets: white and sentinel in the wider margins. More track, and a solitary oxen whipped onwards into the evening.

The men opposite my berth produce a blanket which is spread out over their knees and the gap between the berths. The blanket held taut at the corners, they flick playing cards inwards in a highly charged game of Trumps. The cards are worn at the edge; bright reds and dark blacks collide inwards before a sharp shuffle and a spinning deal.

After each round there is laughter and a mutual reckoning of the scores. One of the younger boys notices my interest and whispers something quickly to his father. The older man looks up, smiles and beckons me to join. I smile back but wave my refusal. He seems to understand.

The game fades into evening as the lights flicker on in the carriage. The pulse of the train, moving forward and swinging sidewards, maintains a constant rhythm of motion and noise. People begin to prepare for the night. Bunks are lowered. There is a steady stream to the toilet, which casts its own insistent mephitic odour along the corridor.

The card players play a last hand before unpacking an evening meal. Tiny parcels of rice and potato wrapped in thick chapati are revealed and shared. Stubby fingers enthusiastically grasp the dhal-stained rice.

I unpack two dried parathas.

As the food settles I slide into a half-sleep of moving stations that drift by in voices and a chorus of offers. Cockroaches scuttle across the dust: unpaid cleaners. A man sings, voice rising, then fading to an evening's lament. Stalls for no reason. People moving; leaving.

I wake to a flickering light in the bunk above the carriage door. I see a face; then it is gone. I turn to face inwards. A teasing of absence, then a slap of shock. The rucksack is only a space.

My hands draw desperately under the bunk scattering cups, dust and cockroaches but nothing else. Then the ease of movement, and I gasp for a belt that is no longer there.

The tighter, stronger gushing of panic begins to flood the adrenaline. My head spins without a stable thought. A rush of ideas and possibilities.

I burst into the compartment of the men and begin turning the cases that are stacked on the floor. Voices in anger and surprise surround me in a language I don't need to understand. I shout back.

71

Lights begin flickering to life in other sections of the carriage. I realise they haven't taken anything and edge out.

A guard arrives. Shouting in Hindi, arms waving, concerned but not conciliatory.

'My rucksack, it's been stolen,' I yell pointing at the empty space. 'Rucksack.' I strike my shoulders aggressively. The guard is three inches away, and he shouts back. I catch nothing.

'He says calm down, he will report it at the station.' The translation is from the card player who had noticed my interest earlier. I wheel on him.

'It'll be too late then.'

The man smiles at me as my anger soars.

'Tell him it'll be too late.'

He reluctantly translates. There is another burst of Hindi. I swear viciously to myself.

'He says we will be at Gorkapur soon, then he will report it. There is nothing he can do now.'

'Search the carriage.'

'He cannot, he does not have the authority.'

'Shit.' I stare into the dark eyes of the guard. I know it's not him I hate. I feel the engine begin to ease as the first sporadic street lights of the new town fly past the window, then the wheels break as the buildings thicken to the centre of a town. The guard rushes to the carriage door as the platform appears. All the lights are now on in the carriage and all eyes are on me. I am the entertainment.

The door is thrown back and the first chai seller is barred by the guard. He beckons me forward. The train is surrounded by a horde of hawkers selling tea and peanuts. Hands are thrust through the windows seeking a sale. I reach the door at the same time as a soldier from the platform. He points a rifle at me. There is an absurd reaction to lift my hands which I can't resist. He smiles and shakes his head, beckoning me onwards with his rifle. I notice it has a wooden barrel and a bolt lock. I can't take my eyes from the darkness of the steel.

The platform is vast and empty after the cage of the carriage. Only hawkers, and they drift away from us as the soldier leads me along. I notice the details: the heavy fall of the man's boots, a cockroach flat and lifeless, a beggar curled and old, a sign in script, Gorkapur. The station clock. It is after four. Eyes stare out through the bars of the train. A man and a soldier.

He leads me to a guard's room at the far end of the station. A single room, a covered desk, timetables and directives on the walls. Other soldiers have appeared. One directs me to sit in the chair facing the desk. The fan on the ceiling turns sluggishly. I ask about the train. Is it going to leave? Soldiers shake their heads. I can just see the last carriage through the door. They appear to be waiting for someone. Orders? A door to an anteroom swings open and the soldiers stop talking. The officer is obviously tired; his shirt hangs loose and open over a brown vest. Trousers slack and unbuttoned. He barely looks at me as he straddles his chair. Then he gestures with a lazy hand.

'Stolen?'

'Yes a rucksack, from the train, I was sleeping, then...'

He waves a hand to stop my burst of words.

'That is a very bad train, many things stolen.' He appears about to elaborate but contents himself with a turn of his hands.

'You have to make a report. But perhaps not here. Tomorrow, at Agra Cant.'

'But it'll be too late then.'

He laughs to himself.

'Too late, too late for what?'

A tap on my shoulder spins me around. The train is moving. I dive for the door. It's fifty yards down the platform but has yet to pick up speed. I am conscious of nothing but the need to reach the train. Boots hitting the platform hard and fast. The blur of night flying past. The green retreating back. No thought of breath as flight sucks me on. Urging my legs, sight fixed. Brushing through hawkers, past sleeping beggars, catching the train. There's a figure at the door. Arms waving me on, then grasping as I judge the speed before making the leap. I fall forward into the carriage. Chest rising; forcing air back in. The breathing eases with the climb of the train pushing on.

I look up; it is my translator. His eyes consider me, searching for something, an explanation perhaps? Then he smiles, a wide, easy, amused smile before proffering a cigarette. I take it without thought.

This Time of Year

It had been a late night. The tight, cloying smell of the bar had followed him home. He could still taste it on his lips; lingering, a thickness that baffled any flow of clear thought.

Steve blinked hard before pushing the quilt back. Michelle stirred on the far side of the bed; heavy thighs and hips pushed up under the sheets smudging her shape.

She turned over towards him, eyes shut, dark hair tousled around her face. He smiled as he always did when he saw her sleeping. Still vulnerable. Still the trusting girl he married five or six years back. She'd put on a bit of weight. Most of them did that, especially after children.

They were still waiting for a second baby; every month she counted the days only to slump back disappointed with the reality of her period. Another child would mean spreading the money further, but he could see the sense in it. She had grown up in a family of four. He was an only child.

He pushed himself up, peering at the bedside alarm clock. He had forty minutes before he needed to be on the slip road outside Manion's.

Michelle's hand grasped for him as he stood up. Clutching in the half-light, then falling back to sleep again. She would be tired from being awake with Daniel in the night. He could half remember the insistent scream, a light in the corridor, Michelle's

79

voice, silence, then nothing until he felt her weight slip back in beside him.

He cast himself a glance as he passed the wardrobe mirror. Heavy, muscled legs, arms thick and firm; only his stomach showed the Saturday beer which was becoming too regular. He always drank too much at this time of year. The weather depressed him, low skies that never lifted above the mountains. Thick banks of water hugging the hills, coating everything in a wet sheen that would linger until the summer. The summer would be fine, light extending further into the evenings, and he could make long runs along the river or drive down to the city with Michelle and Daniel. This year Daniel would be big enough for the beach at Porthcawl.

The boy was awake when he reached the side of the cot; looking up, expecting his mother, but this face would do.

He had changed him and was breezing through a breakfast when Michelle appeared from the bedroom. She offered him a brief smile, half awake, half asleep. Not too pleased that he'd been out late drinking but grateful for his trying to help with Daniel. He didn't try too often, but he did try. It was more than many of the others she knew about.

'Tea ?'

She nodded in reply, stooping to kiss her son. The

soft, slow morning sounds of a family stirring filled the kitchen. Voices on the radio, water running, then boiling, chair legs on a tiled floor.

'Going to your mother's this afternoon?'

Michelle nodded at him. She knew she couldn't keep it up for long. It wasn't worth it. He had not returned that late or that drunk. Just late and drunk. Another Wednesday at the Dragon forgotten by Thursday. Running into a hundred other Wednesdays twisting back into the future and past of a marriage. Just last night she would have liked him to be home, for the company, someone to talk to. Friends. That's why she married him.

'Are you working this weekend?'

There it was, the silence gone; last night forgotten. He nodded, then added: 'Is that okay?'

'Yeh, just checking, Jo asked if I would like to go down to Cardiff on Saturday.'

'You going?'

'I will now.'

'It's just that I thought we could do with the extra money, the work won't be there for much longer.'

She smiled at him reassuringly, forcing him to grin submissively back.

'I thought you were mad at me.'

'I was, but I'm not now.' She leaned over to kiss him, brushing his cheek, then his nose with her lips. 'Taking me out Friday?' She raised her smile.

'Your mother having Daniel?' The child looked up from his bowl at the mention of his name. Michelle nodded.

'Going to Gran's, yes, I know you are.'

Daniel stifled a giggle, turning away shyly.

'Well I'm taking you out then.'

She kissed him again, quicker but on the lips.

'You'd better be going.'

He looked up at the clock above the door.

'Shit, got to rush.'

He pulled his thick jacket closer to shut out the wind, which still carried cold rain from the south. Another month, then the weather would break. Hang on for the change. Cars flushed past on the road stirring swathes of water, rear lights blinking. He guessed Jeffreys would be late but not too late, not on this foul morning. He only had to drive ten miles, straight down the A470, but he usually managed to be late. He always had a different excuse: another woman, a night at his mother's, couldn't remember where he'd parked the van when the Fleur had shut. Most of them had to be genuine. Jeffreys wasn't that original. And then he was nominally the boss inasmuch as he picked up the contracts.

The white Ford Transit was already waiting in the lay-by when Steve reached it.

'Good morning, Steve.'

'You think so?'

'A fine morning, I can feel we're going to be lucky today, I can sense it. The weather will clear by lunch and we're going to get so much work done it'll be a pleasure to be out; in fact we should be paying the Bay to be there.'

Steve smiled weakly at Jeffreys.

'Late one last night?'

He nodded.

'I had an early night, there was this programme on the telly, all about American prisons in Alabama, high security prisons for people who are never coming out; half of them were on death row. Old folks' homes for murderers, except half couldn't walk or piss properly.'

'Sounds fascinating.'

'It was. The stories... one guy had murdered his whole family in the '50s...'

Steve hunched further into his coat. Allowing the words of a documentary to wash over him.

The van pulled out into the flow of traffic, and Jeffreys pointed it towards the gap in the mountains where the river finally escaped the valley, pushing out to the plain, the Bristol channel somewhere in the distance, fringing the bay.

'I just love the Japanese.' Jeffreys was speaking to himself, but he preferred it that way. Steve flicked through the opening pages of *The Sun* before skipping to the back and reading about Arsenal's one nil win at

Highbury. He followed Arsenal vaguely through the papers; the win would lift them a couple of places. Points they needed. He had supported Arsenal since his first year at Comp. You had to follow someone and Arsenal seemed as good as anyone. They had a few stars, Brady and Big Mac, and the red and white strip was easy to remember. There was the fan club, match of the day, even an endorsed football that had arrived one Christmas. It was a craze, everyone had them. He never considered actually going to see a match. London was another world away in England, irrelevant. The reality of a match had nothing to do with the passion of supporting. Then the craze had faded; he'd drifted away from soccer, giving up on the Keys pub team after an ankle injury picked up on the astro turf. He took up golf, which bored him, then nothing. But he still checked the scores on a Monday morning to see how they had fared on the weekend, an away win at Man City, defeat at Norwich. A win at home to the leaders, a big day. It was a constant, a sense of continuity; people changed, friends moved on or away. He had changed and moved on. He was now a married man a year before thirty with a child and a plan for another, but Arsenal still played every Saturday afternoon between August and May while paying too much for their players.

'Another thing I can tell you about the Japs, they're not over here for nothing.'

Steve looked up at Jeffreys, who handed him a corned beef sandwich.

'Mother made 'em. Can't eat 'em all. That lad from Deers is going for chips, I'll put an order in with him. Do you fancy some?'

'Aye 'ere you are,' replied Steve while squeezing some coins from his pocket.

'Don't worry about that, you can get 'em tomorrow.'

Steve pushed himself off the floor where he had been enjoying the first break of the morning.

'Usual?'

'Aye.'

Jeffreys picked his way across the concrete floor of the soon-to-be-completed office block, avoiding the coils of loose wire and lengths of two-by-four.

'What do you think they'll be doing in here then, Steve?'

'Couldn't tell you.'

They had the contract to fit the partitioning walls. Easy work. There was another floor to finish, then maybe some detail work on the lower floors if he had bid low enough. There was no security but Jeffreys liked it that way; he needed to be challenging someone, pulling something over the big boys, making a thousand or two a job. He and Steve knew the bastards would be making a hundred thousand, but you still had to try it; otherwise they'd really screw you and would always screw you.

They worked through the morning, cutting and fitting. Working quickly and easily knowing each others strengths and lapses. Not talking, half listening to the radio that blurred the background. Steve liked this site, its space and the view to the south, the light changing through the day as the sun brightened the clouds. He liked to watch the herring gulls, scraggy, heavy birds; they cut around the Pier Head building as if it were an old rigger they expected to sail away on the incoming tide.

'Ay there's nothing out there you know.'

Steve pulled himself away from the window.

'I'm not so sure.'

Jeffreys smiled at him.

'You're a dreamer, not a chippy.'

'Can't I be both?'

Jeffreys looked at him hard.

'Another babi on the way?'

'No, not yet. I was thinking of buying a boat and sailing around the world.'

'Not before lunch. I've paid for the chips.'

'Not sure Michelle is too keen on boats though.'

Jeffreys looked out across the bay.

'There's a great view from up here.'

'Time to knock off?'

'Right, I'll see where our bloody chips are.'

Steve watched him head for the stairs before he returned to the view. It was worth coming to this site. Perhaps Jeffreys was right.

'And I'll tell you another thing; they should never have let him out in the first place.'

Jeffreys talked through a mouthful of brown chips swollen with vinegar he had splashed on from his own supply. Steve listened and he didn't; occasionally prompting when Jeffreys looked at him but not really understanding to what he was responding. Some of the other lads reckoned Jeffreys talked too much; they had wagered Steve would not last three months. That was three years ago. No one had honoured the bet, but then they never did. Sure, he talked, but then Steve didn't, and he and Jeffreys got along just fine. One talking, the other listening while they both made money.

He'd worked for Deers before: easy, regular money, overtime but not too much. Just turn up five days a week and take home three hundred on a Friday. Regular and easy, but he didn't really fit in with the humour, the larks and the card games. He could have got by, bared it; there were always a few who did, all the way to retirement. Working their way through life without even stirring the sand. Easy marriage, easy kids, easy retirement. He had guessed he was in for that. Then Jeffreys approached him in the Dragon on a Friday night, come all the way down from Porth claiming he needed a partner; his last had just emigrated to Canada. Promised he'd put him on fifty-fifty straight off. Just needed someone he could rely on; he'd do the paperwork.

The lads at Deers had warned him off. Bill Morris had emigrated to Canada to avoid the bastard, and Jeffreys would talk to the statues in Bute Park if he thought they would stay still long enough to listen. But he worked his week's notice with Deers and was on a new industrial estate outside Cwmbran the following Monday.

So Jeffreys talked; Steve listened and sometimes he didn't. They got on well.

'The lawyers got him out after twenty years, and three weeks later he's done a murder almost exactly like the first one. They should have electrocuted him.' Jeffreys looked over towards Steve who nodded his agreement. Jeffreys thought about his declaration then sharply changed the subject.

'I've got to have a word with Baz this afternoon, see if he's going to give us the finishing work below; think you can finish up this corner?'

Steve looked at him offering his own question.

'I'll slip down now, catch the bastard while he's stuffing his face with another of those pies he's so fond of.'

The afternoon followed. Easy and quiet. They'd clear the target for the week with no problem and clean up on Saturday. Steve guessed Jeffreys had gone in too low on this one, but they could still make five hundred, and if they could get the finishing another couple of thousand.

He paused to watch people move on the site below. Another set of foundations was being traced out of the spoil by a trio of JCBs. More money would be flowing into the Bay. If Jeffreys could keep on the right side of the contractors, they'd have enough work down here for another couple of years at least. It would put a bit of security into the house. Maybe an extension at the back; they'd need an extra bedroom with another child.

Michelle had already booked a fortnight in Cyprus for September. Another six hundred. She was still spending as if she'd forgotten she no longer earned nine hundred a month from the Halifax. She had not wanted to go back after the baby. He didn't mind, just wished she could curb the spending. It was alright before Daniel, they had money then, looking for things to spend it on, but now it just seemed to go, easily, like water through an open hand. New clothes, pushchair, car safety seat; he couldn't believe how much their food bill came to every week. He needed to pull down the overdraft this summer. Fifteen hundred was costing him too much in interest. A week in her parents' caravan in Coney beach would have been fine. But she went there anyway on the weekends he was working. Next year he would insist: foreign holidays were out until he'd cleared the overdraft, no matter how much Michelle wanted a tan.

A roll of insulation tape thudded into the wall that

ran into the window where he was looking out and thinking. Steve jumped back, startled.

'Daydreaming again? Not going to be a millionaire dreaming, Steve.' Jeffreys was beaming, on a high.

'You got it?'

'Yep, we got it.'

'Great.'

'Reckon we'll clear four thousand on that one.'

'How much did you go in for?'

'Eight five.'

'Never.'

'No one else interested; they all guessed we'd sewn it up on the first one anyway. Only Deers put a standard in. They were thousands out.' Jeffreys beamed. He'd pulled one on the bastards and he knew it.

'Reckon I might clear the overdraft on that one.'

'Michelle still spending your pennies is she?'

'What do you think?'

'I think she's an charming, attractive, expensive girl.'

They sauntered through the rest of the afternoon, working quickly before beginning to clear up just after three.

'Fancy a pint in the Packet?'

'Need to get back, I was out late last night.'

'Just the one, promised I'd buy Baz a pint.'

'Just the one?'

'Promise, just the one. We can afford the one on expenses.'

90

The noise of work, constant and stuttering through its many rhythms, swirled around them as they descended the stairwell. Enough hours had been given for the day, and men were beginning to think of the journey home, back to wives and children, mothers and girlfriends.

'Aye Jeffreys you tight bugger,' a big man called across the site. A white hat marked him as someone in charge of others.

Jeffreys recognised the foreman who worked for Deers.

'I'd better go and tell him he was miles out, catch you at the van.'

A man from Deers winked at Steve as he headed out through the swing doors of the expensive new office block. A face he just remembered. Just.

A cold burst of air greeted him at the entrance, shivering from the sea, tousling his hair; he shivered. The rain had stopped.

Doris and Ethanol
on the City Road

You were so fat. Just lying there pale, naked and obese. And you smelled, but I got used to that. You have to, I guess, it's part of the job. I named you Doris Jones, after a lottery winner in the paper. No one had bothered to tell me your real name; it would have been too personal. But that's what I needed, a sense of contact, something tangible. You were real.

At first your sheer size appalled me; how could you have consumed that much? Then it became a challenge; none of the others were as fat as you. If I could do it with you, a thin body would be no problem. Learning quickly, I guarded your secrets possessively. No one would come this close again.

As our weekly meetings stretched into December, our awkwardness lessened, your stiffness decreased as you became malleable to my requests, my eager hands, stained and tight with nerves. We became friends. Thursday mornings became a haven from the rest of the week; the reality of all that false contact. I could rely on you being there, waiting for me, slowly revealing your secrets, of your glands and the drinking, but the real knowledge came later.

We lived on the City Road. You were alone except for two cats. Both named after your late husband, dead for nine years. Occasionally, in the tired light of an early Sunday morning you still heard him grumbling about the football results and the pools forecast. He had spent the last twenty years waiting for the win to end his problems. It was a coronary in the end. Arthur and Jonsey were more than adequate replacements.

The house had come with your winnings. It was a hollow street peopled by employees and students who always found excuses to be away at the weekends. There was a stiff feeling of unease which permeated the houses and the people as they rushed from cars into doorways, desperately avoiding each other in case they were tricked into conversation. Once it had been a street to move to, a proper address, but now the houses ached from neglect, bought for renting by landlords who had moved to the suburbs or Spain. You existed through the rash of removal and arrival, resigned but disappointed. You collected things that the students threw out, old CD players, pillowcases, suitcases, lamp stands. Your house bulged with used things, objects of want no longer wanted. You couldn't understand why they threw such valuable things away. You grew bigger with food and untold secrets, waiting for someone to cut them out. Perhaps you knew it was going to be me. There was certainly no objection. Your breasts were so huge, they slumped to the side. I compared them to my own, small and dark. But we were told to ignore the skin. We would study that again. It would be preserved.

As I got deeper, another, more subtle smell, emerged from under the ethanol. A darker, fermented taste of rye, oak and burnished adverts in Sunday print. Your liver, swollen and cavitous, confirmed your vice.

Drinking was a solace; practiced fiercely on Saturday afternoons as the racing faded into results, before the inevitable game show became hilarious or depressing, depending on the brand. Sunday morning arrived in a cold, uneasy blur as you dragged yourself from the sofa to a cold, comfortless bed. My Sundays were spent with my own reports. I swallowed paracetamol in your memory in an attempt to disinfect the taste of borrowed smoke and beer exchanged in fumbling embraces on my own unmade bed. The men had usually sneaked away by the morning. A sober, daylight encounter would have been too much to bear with the scents still strong, but all desire pissed away with the beer.

The afternoon would find me reading while you were still slumbering; ignoring an insistent bladder which would eventually force you downstairs for a piss and a cold meat tea. The others laughed as your bladder, huge and bloated, moved of its own volition across the board as I touched it. My friends laugh silently now as they stick to the kitchen wall, wrapped in cocktail dresses and smiles before they fade into the next tenant and the bottom of my own battered suitcase. Sometime, someone will unlock them in an attic: still smiling, dusty but ageless.

A picture of your son in the hallway confronted the few visitors who called. He was secure in his framed smile from a safe distance. He lived in Southampton. He provoked memories of a cider-laden summer afternoon and a County cricket match. Then a quick, expectant pregnancy as he swelled inside you. It would be the last. A careless surgeon provoked an infection that took another two to clear. The knife scars were still there. My supervisor picked at them with a scalpel before calling the class over for an explanation and discussion. My insides tensed as we talked about advances in technique.

Nights of cider and sex were forgotten in the rush of his childhood. Arthur didn't seem to mind; maybe he found someone else, but you didn't really care. Sex had always involved facing away. I was struggling to get it right myself. I sympathised. Men want you, then they don't.

Your son was a careless, clumsy boy, demanding but vague, who drifted away with no clear intention except to leave. The last postcard was from Weymouth; he did not attend the funeral.

At the end he became easier to contact than you would have anticipated. He knew the value of the house, and he had never been that far away from the City Road. There were no objections to our requests. We would pick up the expenses, and it was always your wish to help science, he maintained. The house moved quickly onto another anonymous tenant.

Death had come easily; unheralded and unambitious. Sliding in slowly one mid-week afternoon. The TV still playing, the paper boy unpaid. You had been found by a man from the Council. I suggested a cerebral haemorrhage; the supervisor agreed. He had only just accepted you; another night and your son would have had to pay the fees himself. Apparently he is offered a lot of corpses. He can choose, but there is a limit to what the ethanol will preserve. For me now it has preserved a year. A time of Doris and I on the City Road. As I sit here staring at what's left of her – a face cut and peeled away – I wonder when I will become a face on my next City Road, hiding away the weeks, salting the weekends.

To the Centre
of the Volcano

I

I'm writing this play. It's set here in Almeria. Two or three characters. I'm not sure yet. We were happy here once. We drove down with the boy when he was eight months old. We were always good at escaping. She was sick for two days on the ferry. It doesn't affect me. I lie down and I'm okay. Then there was Spain. A whole country stretching out before us into the February rain. The last weeks of winter.

We cut south, avoiding the toll roads, and got caught in a snowstorm on the road beyond Teruel. Two days in a truckers' stop with an eight-month-old baby. I can remember a boar's head above the fireplace with a can of Heineken stuffed between its jaws. Bullfighters lined the central beam. The pictures overexposed. The colours fading. Each with his own moment. A TV sat in the far corner. The storm had cut the signal. The barman had tried a few times to get a reception, then gave up, shutting off the power in disgust.

We drank cerveza with fish from under the tapas glass. Atun, cabaya, boquerones: eyes cooked dead or cut into chunks. A basket of bread accompanied each order. By nine we were drunk and Malena's eyes sparkled in the lights. The last year had been hard for her. Her work had not gone well. Two months after the birth she had burned all her materials. I could smell

103

the paint, lingering around the cottage on the hill. The people of the valley distrusted us. We wouldn't be there long. They were right.

The snow rushed against the window, drifted against the shattered lorries in the truck park. The men looked at us keenly. The baby, blond and bright, watched everything. I could see it in their eyes: we were once like that, young men lost in a snowstorm with a wife and child. And look at us now. Old men with responsibilities, a job, a truck to drive.

The next day the snow stopped. I sat around the bar trying to recover from a hangover. Malena spent most of the day in the room. Joshua was hungry. I could hear his cries along the corridor. Most of the truckers had left by mid-afternoon, but we booked in for another night.

Spain was still new again. I hadn't been back since a package tour with my mum and dad twenty years before. The language was a challenge. I pointed at the food under the glass. A man begged a cigarette from me. He walked with a limp. One leg was twisted shorter than the other. He was an old man who had spent a life in the fields, and the sun had been burned into his skin. He smoked desperately, as if trying to ward a spirit away from his lungs. He hobbled back to the bar with his prize.

Malena had needed to get away. She claimed the world was closing in on her. No one would let her show her work anymore. She didn't want to play the game. Art was for wankers. I hoped Spain would see us together again. Anything to escape another Cardiff winter.

The country was new. I thought we had a good chance. We just needed somewhere to let us live for a while. We just had to keep going. Find somewhere.

We had caught the end of Semana Santa in Mazarrón. It was the first week of April and the air was warm. The sea a forever blue. We walked along the promenade mixing with the crowds, the boy in a pushchair we had bought in a charity shop in Granada.

The restaurant advertised a local climatizado. One waiter served the tables on the promenade. A plastic sheet protected the customers from the wind and spring thunderstorms.

The waiter could speak German, good English and some Dutch. French he would not do. His grandfather had died in France during the Second World War. To the French he spoke in heavy Spanish.

The restaurant served patatas bravas, squid, mussels and sardines, beer and wine. It would not serve chips and coffee. The waiter offered us the menu of the day. We said we wanted the tapas and beer. He said that was okay, but the menu of the day would have been better.

He struggled with the rush of customers driven off the promenade by the rain. His voice sharp in three languages and the shouting in Spanish. The cook pushed the heaped plates out to him through a window in the wall. He carried a paper table covering over to us and managed a flourish of English as he set the table.

'Would you like to move, inside?'

Malena shook her head.

'The rain is going to be heavy.'

'We like it here.'

'It is okay, here is good. Inside would be better, but here is good.'

Malena smiled thinly at him.

'Are you ready to order?'

Malena looked at me. It was my turn to order. I always made a mess of ordering. We never got what I asked for.

'Patatas bravas?'

He nodded. I struggled on.

'Un patatas bravas, un tortilla, one menu del la dia.'

The waiter smiled. 'No problem.' He scurried back into the restaurant.

Malena grinned at me. I made excuses.

'It was easier.'

'You don't know what you are getting.'

'There's wine with it and bread.' I pointed at the board.

'There might be meat. What's huelones?'

'It doesn't matter. I'll eat it anyway.'

'You always do.'

'What's wrong with that?'

'You always compromise.'

I looked out across the promenade to where the water had turned from blue to grey as the clouds covered the sky. The first drop of rain began to hit the plastic awning. The boy shuffled in his pushchair, still asleep, dreaming.

We watched the procession as it merged at the Church of San Juan. Serious young men in purple satin robes struggling with a statue of the Virgin. She looked white as if sick with the unsteady motion of the carnival parade.

A marching band followed, echoing into a night sky scythed with swifts. The devil birds laughing at the humans and their follies. We bought a balloon for Joshua, and his eyes opened wide with delight, looking up into the yellow night.

The parade seemed to follow us around town as we moved from bar to bar drinking. She could always match my drinking. I miss the competition of it, the free carousing. By twelve we were drunk and the boy was asleep again. We walked back down the promenade. People lingered with the night. Holding onto the holiday. A crowd was gathered looking at the beach. The flickering lights of candles played on the sand. As we walked closer we could see the sculptures. Beautifully crafted out of the sand, and then coloured with food dyes. A virgin in sand, a cathedral with spires, Jesus with a halo, and taking centre stage, Homer Simpson and his family. They were sitting on a sand settee watching a sand television. A real rug in front of them collected donations from the holiday crowd, *gracias* printed out on the sand. It was the work of a real sculptor, even here in the sand. I could see the hours that had been spent on acquiring the skill. I turned to Malena, looking for her smile at the work, but there was only the crowd. Then panic thudded into me as I saw her jump the wall onto the beach. The sculptor had seen her but he was too slow. Bart got it first. His yellow head shattered into a thousand grains as Malena's fist connected with it. Then Homer and Marge. I was there by then with the sculptor. I thought he was going to hit her but he only shouted. The crowd bayed at us, and Malena was kicking and biting me trying to get at the rest of the Simpsons. I dragged her back as the abuse roared around us. Someone threw a bottle, which bounced off my shoulder. Then we reached the pram and the abuse stopped. The baby was crying. Then there was just pity. I held Malena tightly; she cried into my shoulder.

I was driving back to the campsite before she spoke again.

'It's all fucked up. All of it. White virgins and sandcastle Christs. All fucked up.'

The Autovía del Sur is a bleak road, but it has the feel of escape.

Two weeks later, we were still driving. We were running out of money and things to say to each other. We had stopped at a square in San José and the Englishman found us. He became our first friend in Spain. He had been a shepherd in the Pyrenees, but now he ran an antique shop. He couldn't walk very far now. He had an abscess on his spine. He swam along the front of the village beach in the mornings. He had spoken to Malena in the shop. She was dark, and he had tried Spanish, then Portuguese. The Englishman knew the country. We should walk up into the centre of the volcano.

He had a house in the village. We were welcome to the spare room. We could share his bills. Malena stopped trying to imagine herself somewhere else. We were here. Now.

We promised him we would walk to the volcano

It took us three weeks to get around to it.

The path cut down through Las Presillas Baja. The village was strewn across a spur above the dry valley pouring out from the volcano. We walked on the loose coarse sand which marked the floor of the rambla. The Englishman had said it was an hour's walk at most. We found the going hard. The boy was heavy. Ten pounds at birth and three times that now. We had squashed him into my rucksack and tied him in. His eyes followed the valley at first, but he soon fell asleep and lolled forward, pulling on my back.

We stopped after an hour. A rusted frame of a car lay abandoned in the centre of the path. Sand and rock had washed around it.

Malena sat on the boot of the car. I remember thinking what was a car doing so far from the road. A lost cause, dreams given up.

She looked away from me, up across the scrub of the mountain. The core of a volcano thrown out thirty million years ago. And now we were here. Two tourists and their child climbing to its centre. Our feet light on the dry, flaking earth.

'Why do you think they gave up on it?'

I lowered the boy from my back, not wanting to answer her. She could see the car as clearly as I could. It was a used-up thing.

'It was an insurance claim. They drove it up here and hoped no one would find it?'

'All this way?' She brushed some dust from the bonnet of the car. It would have been red once but now it had faded to brown in the sun, and rivers of rust ran down from the cracks in its body panels. All the windows had gone and the seats were piled high with rocks.

Her shorts rose high on her legs. The boy snored lightly. She smiled at me. She wanted to play the game.

'Alright, there were three French tourists, Hugo, Muriel and I forget the other one.'

'Haj.'

'Ok, Haj. He was a Moroccan. They took the wrong

turning in the village and were trying to get to Rodalquilar.'

She smiled at me, flicking her hair back. A sand grouse called from the scrub. The heat surrounded us. I gently put the boy on the ground in the shade of the Fiat. His arms flexed once into the air, grasping for me, before he fell back into sleep. She waited for me.

'Hugo was married to Muriel but in love with Haj.'

'He couldn't find a way to tell her...?'

'They drove up into the hills and?' She waited for me. It was a game to finish first.

But it had to be good.

'Threw her into the well at the ruined farmhouse.'

'That's rubbish.'

'Best I could do.'

'It doesn't explain the car.'

She looked away up into the dry hills. Nothing moved. I could see the disappointment on her face. I was close to her now, facing her. She put her arms around me. I kissed her once. Then once again, longer. I could feel the heat on my back run through me. The heat of the car in the sun on my thighs. The softness of her legs, bare and brown. I traced a line with my fingers along the inside of her leg. My fingers touching soft, light skin. She curled her hands around my back. I moved my hand up onto her breast. They were round, still full with milk. I could feel her nipples harden beneath her T-shirt, beneath my fingers. My dick pushed out against the hard cotton of my shorts. The heat of the day filled the valley. She pulled my hand down and looked away.

'Do you think she's in the well?'

'Yeh, of course.' I followed her gaze. The vapour trail of a jet cut across the blue sky before fading out high to the south.

'I'm sorry. It's just that...'

'It doesn't matter.'

The boy stirred beneath us. His feet scuffing the sand.

II

Spain is very big. It took ages to get where Dad wanted to go. We kept stopping in places he didn't want to stay in. We did see some castles and huge bulls made out of wood. Dad said they were advertising a drink. But he didn't know what drink and we never bought it.

The play isn't making much progress. The Englishman isn't here anymore. The man who runs the restaurant claims he could be living with a woman in Bilbao. I needed to speak to him again. I wanted to put him in the play. I hope to drink alone now.

The bar is called Calle Piscina. Nothing special. Six plastic trestle tables and a blue awning to shield the sun. Inside, wooden tables, a straight counter with a glass display case keeping the flies from the potatoes and sardines.

The girl who serves doesn't try very hard. The first day she raised a smile, laughed with Joshua, but after three weeks I've become a fixture. She doesn't smile and shouts at the boy in Spanish when he scurries under the table for his ball. It is out of season and she imagines she shouldn't be serving tables in Las Presillas, a dried-out village in the desert. I think she's a girlfriend of the cook, but whenever they are together a fever curses the tables and the customers evaporate into the dusty village.

113

The boy's given up on the ice creams. For the first week he wanted ice cream three times a day but now the taste has tired him and he just asks for water. I wish I could give up on the wine.

Joshua looks up at me, trusting. I know it is time to finish this. We have been here too long now.

Dad drinks red wine. He can order red wine. Dad drinks a lot of red wine. Then he starts telling jokes and sometimes he cries. Dads shouldn't cry. People stare at us. Dad just sitting there and crying. But he says he doesn't care. He's crying for Mam. He shouldn't cry for Mam. Mam's dead. I don't cry for Mam anymore. Grandma Porthcawl said Mam was in a better place. Dad doesn't believe in God. Grandma Porthcawl said that's why he cries. She said Dad wasn't going to get me back. But he did. It wasn't his fault, whatever Grandma Porthcawl says.

The police called yesterday to check my papers. There had been a request to confirm that I was okay. If the boy was okay. I could see the disdain in the officer's eyes. The squalor we were living in. I've never been good at housework. It was one of her complaints. I came home once and we didn't have a plate left in the house. She said she was sick of washing them, and if I wasn't going to do it we could eat with our hands off paper every night. She had given it all away. Every dish, fork, spoon, pan in the house to the charity shop

114

on Clifton Street. I tried to buy some of it back. There was a set of my grandmother's best Spode. I got four pieces. Two cups, a cracked plate and a saucer. The rest had been sold. Serves me right, she said. I kept those washed until she broke them.

'You stay here long?' The policeman's eyes caressed the mess in the apartment. Unwashed plates, strewn clothes, pieces of food on the floor.

'No, un meses, maybe dos.'

He looked around again. He didn't like trouble. He wasn't used to it. Some drunks and some people hitting each other, usually family. He could handle that. I was trouble, tourist trouble. His orders had come from Málaga and from there Madrid. The consulate had become involved. He didn't like being told what to do.

He checked my passport, then Joshua's. Joshua was eight months old in the passport photograph. He was being held by his mother. It was the first time we came away. The officer folded them back together and passed them back.

'Mr Hones, your passports are fine. We are a European country. Civilised. The boy will be old enough for school. Here it is free.' He searched for the right word. 'And... mandatory.'

He waited for a reaction. Joshua came in from the bedroom. The police had called early. He edged back into the shadows. Afraid of strangers.

'Me hable… en el pueblo.'

'Yes, you will speak to someone, but in Almeria. Not here. He can go to the school in El Pozo.'

'In September?'

'But you will not be here in September, un mesa no?'

'Si.'

'Then maybe we don't have a problem.'

'No, I don't think so.'

He looked around the place once more and then spoke to himself.

'Viven como cerdos… pero qué import?'

Dad said the volcano was in the mountains. We could climb to the centre when we had a day of good weather. The weather has been good for ages. It's hot and sunny. Sunny and hot. It's always hot and sunny. Last week we had lightning in the night but no rain. The rain doesn't like the coast.

It's a promise. I have to stick to it. We get up early; the sun is still struggling to fill the slopes of agave and prickly pear with enough light for us to see by. The rambla has a different light. The shadows play with your imagination. Joshua has brought Scorch along for protection. Scorch is a dragon. A cloth dragon filled with beans. Scorch is going to protect Joshua from the wolves and wild boar. I've tried to tell him there are no wolves in this part of Spain. They've all been shot.

Joshua is a good walker now. He doesn't complain. I can feel the heat on my body, straining. The wine gets to you quickly. I can feel my weight filling me up again. I haven't eaten much since the summer. There didn't seem much point, need. Now it's the wine.

It takes us an hour to reach the farmhouse. We sit down and eat bread and cheese with some apricots. The well is covered up. A lattice of pine posts laid across its mouth to protect the foolish. We call down, listening for the words to expand and reform in the depths. I wonder if the French tourist is still down there, listening.

The rambla curves on, always at the bottom of the valley, caressing its way to the centre of the volcano. We reach the Fiat. This was as far as the three of us got the first time. The sun was too hot for us. We had not brought enough water. January is cooler, the skies deeper. There are just two of us.

Joshua clambers up onto the bonnet and then onto the roof.

'It's a car.' He looks down at me. 'Why hasn't it got any windows?'

'It's been abandoned.'

'No tyres, no seats, no anything.' He heaves a rock from the top of the car into a thicket of prickly pear. He looks hard at the car, considering it. 'Can we mend this car? We could go home then?'

'I don't think so.'

117

'Can we mend our car?'

'No.'

'Why hasn't our car got an engine? This car has got an engine.'

I had to agree with him. The car did indeed have an engine.

Our car is sitting in the village square with its engine missing. Dad asked someone to fix it for him. The man said he had to take the engine away. That was a long time ago. Dad lets me sit in the car sometimes while he drinks in the bar. The radio doesn't work anymore. Dad reckons it's because the battery is flat but I think it's because the engine is missing. The car is full of things from home. I found my lion in it on Monday. The lion had been missing since the ferry. Dad said I must have left it in the cabin but I didn't take it to the cabin. I left the lion in the car to guard it. I found it between the seats with a chocolate wrapper and some raisins. I ate the raisins. They were a bit dusty.

We push on up the rambla as the heat begins to seep down from the volcano. A hare skips across the broken rocks. Then, where the valley deepens, a line of almond trees. They are just flowering, a pink-washed white pouring out from the dry rambla.

This will be the place I had imagined. It will be okay for us. Below the trees there is an old squared field. Green shoots rise up from softer earth.

118

Dad said she was very sick when we visited her in hospital. She looked very sick. She couldn't speak to us. Then I woke in Grandma's house. She said Mam was in a better place. She didn't say where Dad was.

I unpack the rucksack I've been carrying. The camping spade unfolds easily. It was designed for burying your shit in the woods. The soil is soft. I begin to dig. Joshua watches.

'What are you doing, Dad?'

I don't answer, just keep digging. There is no point in asking questions now. I can't talk my way out of this. The hole is about three feet deep when I stop. I think that is enough. Just enough.

Joshua has wandered off. He's trying to dig up some shoots with a stick. I call him over. He looks up, sensing something. I see the fear in his eyes. I wasn't expecting this. I thought I had worked everything out.

Then it hits me. A hard, searing pain shoots through my leg, and I fall heavily into the dirt. The hole looms up to greet me. The earth is thrust up into my eyes and nose. A clatter of legs and a rich smell of dried sweat and bristle runs over me.

I'm three feet down and scrabbling at the sides. I come up for air quickly. The pig has stopped for breath. Joshua is screaming. Caught in the moment, unable to move. The pig is sizing us up. Which one? Joshua is smaller, easier.

I stumble forward, slipping on the earth, scrambling to get to him first. I smother tackle him as the pig hits us again. I can hear the breath in her lungs. Fear. Then squeals.

I pick Joshua up and run for the almond tree. The pig, stalled by the sudden movement, hesitates but then kicks into the ground again and rushes for us.

With six feet to go I hurl Joshua into the lower branches. They crack and splinter but he hangs on in fear. The adrenaline fires through me as I jump for the trunk and heave myself up into the tree. The tree sways with my weight. A shower of almond blossoms falls to the ground. The pig grunts around twice at the base of the tree. The tree sways unsurely. I watch her as she looks around sniffing, her glands extended with milk. A squeal from the bushes calls her back into the thicket of prickly pears.

I can feel my heart crashing through my ribs, the red wine surfacing in sweat. Joshua clambers across the branches to me. He's not crying. He loves trees. I hug him to me.

His head breaks free. He wants to speak.

'I told you Scorch would protect us.' He is still holding the cloth dragon.

'Yeah, lucky we had Scorch.'

'What's the hole for, Dad?'

I look at him. His blue eyes, my eyes, his nose, my nose. His mind all his own.

'Your mother.'

I pour her ashes into the hole under the almond tree. Joshua helps me fill in the loose earth. Then we run in case the pig comes back.

We didn't stay long in Spain after that. I sold the carcass of the car. Twenty thousand pesetas. We just had enough to catch the train back from Almeria.

The ferry was huge. The sea surrounded us but we couldn't touch it. Dad said people just went on the ferry for a cruise and wouldn't even get off in Spain unless they were forced to. I loved the playroom. I was the oldest there except Dad. Dad spent all his time in the playroom. He was seasick. He couldn't get off the floor for very long without lying down again.

There was a woman supposed to be organising games for us. There was a list on the wall of all the things we were supposed to do. She only came to see us the first day. She had blond hair and a blue uniform.

She didn't come again. Dad said she was seasick too. I liked the playroom. It reminded me of home.

The Stars Above the City

The piano was old. The lid shut, smeared with dust. Thin light cut into the foyer from the bay beyond. Anthony had spent months dreaming of the Intercontinental. Its green shuttered terraces looking down onto the port. He had arrived at the site of one of his dreams.

A porter appeared and picked up his rucksack. It was light and the man smiled. He indicated that Anthony should follow him. The hotel opened out along wide corridors. He noticed with some disappointment that the carpets were worn, and there were prints of palaces on the walls and an English huntsman with hounds. The room was on the second floor. It opened onto a balcony guarded by iron railings. He looked out over the bay, which curved away to the south. There were fishing boats out beyond the headland. The porter was waiting in the room. Anthony fumbled in his pocket. He only had euros. The man smiled. He passed him two euros.

'Euros are good here.'

He waited for the stillness of the room to reach him. He wasn't quite ready to face the city again, but he had promised a man at the port who claimed to be a good guide – 'official, sir' – to meet him at 5pm. There was enough time to sleep. He tried to imagine himself back, as the sounds of the port rose up past the balconies. Gulls, lorries reversing, a ship leaving. The sounds of a world moving.

125

He woke to a loud knocking at the door. He spun, unsure of the room. His hands grasping at the sheets. Then his memory caught him. He waited as his heart calmed. There was a knock again.

'Monsieur, your guide?'

He was aware of his crumpled trousers and shirt as he answered the door. He blinked at the porter. The sun was hurting his eyes.

'Dix minutes, d'accord?'

The porter smiled and turned away.

The medina proved more than expected. More than he had read about. He didn't realise that a return to the past could be so swift. A surge of life swept into him. The flux of people, living, eating, working in the shaded passages cut out of what seemed the solid life of the city. He had a few offers of things he didn't need but the guide seemed to deflect most of the attention. He appeared to know many of the people who smiled at him. It seemed he had been telling the truth about being an official guide. The guide's name was Mohammed. At least it was one of his names. Anthony suspected he had used it as the easiest one a European might pronounce. He was an old man. Over sixty with tight-cut silver hair. He wore a well-tailored suit and carried an umbrella to protect himself from the sun. He kept it furled in the medina but carried it with a quiet grace that seemed to protect him from the rush of the city.

Mohammed recommended a restaurant and waited while Anthony was served a 'traditional meal'. He was the only customer of the restaurant.

'You are too early for dinner and too late for lunch, but we'll serve you anyway,' the waiter laughed.

The tour continued after the meal.

'It is quiet in the afternoon. Evenings are better. Now people rest. But I will take you to an emporium.'

At the emporium he was introduced as 'Mr Anthony', as if they should know who he was. A silver tray carrying a heavily sugared glass of mint tea was presented to him. He sipped delicately. He wasn't sure of the etiquette. There must be an etiquette. He was invited to sit down as the theatre of carpets was revealed to him. A thrilling display of four different types of rug and carpet was presented by a tall lithe man in a black singlet. His muscles flexed as he unfurled each new display. The commentary was provided by the head of the emporium. Anthony kept his eyes down, trying not to give himself away. He wanted to buy a carpet. It would look good in the flat. There was more space now. He wondered what Jac would have done. Anthony had never been good with salesmen. They sensed a weakness in him. A desire to please. To be helpful almost whatever it cost him. He looked at the man in the vest. There was a sheen on his skin from the heat even in the cool of the emporium. But he knew he simply couldn't buy a carpet on his first

127

day. He bought a blanket. It was the cheapest woollen item in the shop. The man who had served him the tea shook his head sadly as he took his money. He could sense that what Anthony really wanted was a full-scale, two-hundred-and-fifty-thousand knot, five hundred euro carpet. Jac always said he wasn't assertive enough, didn't make demands. Anthony had always found when he made demands he lost things, friends, lovers. He had lost Jac. Jac would have bartered the carpet down to two hundred euros and made the salesmen feel he was doing them all a favour by buying it from them.

He paid the guide off after the third carpet shop.

He followed one of the alleyways back to centre of the medina. It was a Sunday night and children were playing football in the small spaces between the houses. As he walked he had glimpses of lives he could never see in the veiled portals, warm kitchens, the flavours of food high in the air.

He remembered their kitchen in Cardiff. He had loved to fill it with recipes from countries he had never visited as if with alchemy he could produce them to share on order. He loved the programmes on the television that told you how to eat and live. He liked that. He liked the surety of it.

The night was beginning to fold around the city. He walked down the Petit Socco. The chairs were filled with dark men looking out at the moving street, just looking. A shudder went through him. He found a chair at Café Tingis. He looked out. Watching. Men in hooded gowns, women clothed tightly against the world of men, pale Europeans in the coloured clothes of the young and rootless.

A waiter brought him a coffee. He had asked for it in French. He could order food in French. It was a small miracle of his education that he could actually remember words from a classroom twenty years before. The evening filled in the spaces. He began a postcard in his mind. Dear Jac, On the Petit Socco, you would like it here... Dark men with smiles in their eyes. I'm speaking French badly again... sorry, bad French.

Jac had always laughed at his pronunciation. He would write the postcard in the morning. He should be able to get stamps in the city.

A man in a white shirt smiled at him from the crowd. Anthony smiled back. The man waved and began walking towards him.

Sun filtered into the room early. He remembered the bar he had been persuaded to try for one drink. Hardwood, dusty sawdust floor. The smell of hashish. He checked his face. No marks. He could walk away from this.

He packed quickly. The man at the reception took his money without comment. They had refused his credit card, so he'd been forced to withdraw money from a cashpoint. He walked back up the Petit Socco,

129

through the medina to the new town. It had been new in the 1920s when the French had planned it. There was a Café de Paris, and Café de France, along a Boulevard Pasteur. He was tight with sweat from the climb up the hill with his rucksack. There were no offers in the early morning. It was too early for business. He settled into a dark leather chair and withdrew into an order for black coffee with a croissant. He had always liked croissants since his first visit to Paris as a sixteen-year-old. To him they tasted of opportunity and a delicious sense of guilt in the morning. He had visited the *cimetière* with Jonathan. He was rather horrified when Jonathan produced a lipstick from his pocket, covered his lips with the darkest red and kissed the statue above the grave they had both come to see. He had heard Jonathan stayed in Newcastle after university. They had kept in touch for a few years. It seemed a long way back now.

He wrote a postcard to Jac. It didn't say anything. He signed it, *With love from Anthony, Always*.

The bus was half full. He had expected it to be old and battered, but it was new with good seats and air conditioning. He sat next to a man who spoke good English. He was going to Chefchaouen. He worked for the Banc de Maroc. He was going to explain a new computer system to the manager in Chefchaouen. He usually travelled by train, but there was no train to

130

Chefchaouen. Anthony was glad of the information. The man had two children. His wife was expecting a third. Life was good. You worked hard, you enjoyed life. What did Anthony do? Anthony wasn't sure about that. I write – write what? For the television. Films? No. Not films. I write down ideas for television. Shows. Programmes. You get paid for that? Usually. Are they popular? They don't usually get made – I just come up with the ideas.

The man looked at him. He wrote ideas for shows that never got made.

The open fields passed the windows. Men riding donkeys, sunflowers about to open, a grey reservoir. Travel made him think of home. His work. Jac.

He had started writing plays for the theatre. They had been well received. He was young and the reviewers were generous in small papers. He would get better, write better plays with more complex plots. But he didn't get better. He found that after the third he had very little more to say. He worked for television instead. He wrote treatments for new shows that went into development or were offered to digital channels that no one watched. It had allowed him to live for six years in the city he had shared with Jac. It had paid for holidays to Barcelona and New York. It had never felt like much money. But he was happy. Jac was with him. They had partied. They had friends around to dinner. He felt like he was living the life he had wanted as that sixteen-year-old in Paris.

131

That was nine months ago. Before the money came. A treatment had been made into a show. It was called *Fantasy Shop*. It allowed people to indulge. That was its hook. It had been franchised. He had had to employ an agent, and the agent had employed a lawyer on his behalf. He had earned money. A lot of it, very quickly. There was still a cheque for $260,000 due to be paid. His accountant had suggested waiting until the new financial year to accept payment. His tax bill had frightened him. Surely he couldn't be giving that much money away in tax? Where would he get it from? The accountant had reassured him. Then Jac had left him.

The man took out pictures of his two healthy children. Their bright eyes stared out at the bright lights in the photographer's studio. He noticed they were well lit. The photographer had known how to light children, how to get the best from their youth and clear skin. A kind of hopefulness.

The bus stopped at a service station on the brow of a hill. The man from the bank invited him to share a table.

'My name is Abdul. Yours?'

'Anthony.'

'As in Cleopatra, yes?'

Anthony looked blankly at the man.

'The play. Shakespeare?'

'Sorry, of course. I was... a bit out of context.'

The station was crowded, full with families and travellers. The man from the bank had a certain stature that Anthony found attractive. He seemed at ease. A waiter arrived promptly to take their order. Abdul switched into Arabic to order his food. There was a rush of words Anthony found strangely familiar. The sound of the language was rather beautiful. The two men then looked expectantly at him. There was no menu; the butchered side of a cow hung down from the rafters next to the kitchen. Anthony didn't eat meat. He had given up meat five years before on one of Jac's fad diets. But he had surprised himself and stuck to it, which was more than Jac did.

'The fish is very good. Trout.'

Anthony was grateful for the advice. He smiled up at the waiter.

'*Un poisson, un café au lait, sil vous plaît.*'

The waiter retreated to the kitchen.

'*Parlez-vous français?*'

'*Non. Un peu.*'

'It is a fine language. I lived in Marseille for two years. Before I was married of course.'

'You were able to travel there?'

'To work, yes. *La vie est très cher là bas.*' He looked at Anthony and then added, 'Otherwise it is too expensive.'

'You didn't think of staying?'

'No. Why should I? My family is here. I was a young man. I wanted to see another country, that is all.'

The fish arrived. It was grilled dark under a fine spiced flour.

133

The afternoon lengthened as the bus climbed through the valleys that fed into the mountains. He was surprised how green the land was. He saw people on the land, farmers and shepherds, and they were making the most of the land. Cultivated plots stretched up into the hills. Small herds of goats and sheep tended by a shepherd seemed to be travelling up and down the valley. He had expected Morocco to be red with sand dunes. It was ridiculous, he knew, but everyone had a mental image of a country built on something, words and pictures, and through these the country had been categorised, the deserts, palaces, dark men. He could see the men.

The night in Tanger. The bar was not what he was expecting. The man at Tingis had suggested they should go for a real drink at Deen's.

'My name is Haroun. You will like Deen's. It is for you.'

He knew the name. It was in the *Spartacus* guide: 'Just the most lively place in Tanger. Bank clerks and diplomats. Careful after dark.'

He followed Haroun up the Petit Socco and across the square. The road narrowed, and they cut back on themselves down a side alley. A simple sign marked 'Deen's – Prix 10 Euro'. He thought about turning back. Jac blamed him for giving up on things. He took out his wallet and passed the money to the man on the door. Haroun didn't pay anything. The light was low and a heavy Euro-pop beat pushed through the air. There was red lighting and flashing fairy lights. He could just make out the rows of men sitting at the fringes of the room. He could feel their eyes on him. He shouldn't have come in. Haroun took him to a table.

'I'll get us a drink?'

Anthony nodded and Haroun disappeared into the gloom. The music began to eat into him. He wished himself smaller.

A man sat down opposite Anthony. He spoke in what could have been German. Anthony smiled back nervously.

'You are English?'

Anthony nodded. He had explained too many times the subtle differences between Welsh and English.

'I am sorry. I thought you were German. My name is Rashid.' He smiled.

'Anthony.'

'You are here on vacation.'

'Yes.'

'Good. I like to meet people on vacation. I get to improve my English. I work in a bank. I need to speak to people. You are a very attractive man.'

Anthony blushed. He had never been called that before. People were usually more subtle or honest.

'Do you have a boyfriend in England?'

A waiter arrived with two drinks. They looked like spirits, probably vodka. Anthony took one of the glasses. His new companion waved the waiter away.

'I don't drink. Because I am a Muslim.' He laughed.

135

'Maybe I shouldn't be doing this either.' The man raised his eyebrows in a way that sent a shiver down Anthony's spine. He had never been good at this part of the game. He took a sip of the drink. It was vodka. He then swallowed the remainder. He felt the liquid caress his throat, urging him forward.

In the alley he kissed Rashid. There was no one around. He could feel the urgency in the man's caress. In the club Rashid had been confident but now, back in the reality of his city, he was scared. They could both go to jail for this. As Anthony pushed his hand hard onto the man's cock, he could feel the soft, wet warmth of his semen immediately, the tensing of his body as he came, lost in the desire and finality of the moment. Rashid pulled away.

'I am sorry.'

'It's okay. It's my turn now, though.'

The man shook his head. The situation catching up with him. He straightened his trousers, re-zipping his fly.

'I go now.'

'No, not yet.' The man turned and began walking away. 'You can't.'

But he quickly merged into the shadows. A cat scuttled past him. Anthony looked up. He could see the stars above the city.

Money had always been difficult for Anthony. His father

worked at the steelworks. He had been a chemist. Anthony was twelve before he realised his father had more money than other boys' fathers who also worked at the steelworks. His family holidays were package tours to hot places in Spain he couldn't remember the names of. His father changed the family car every few years for a new model. Always something built by Leyland. His father had attempted to push him towards science. Medicine would have been a good career option. Anthony was 'being offered chances that I couldn't dream of'. Anthony had wanted to go to art college. They compromised; English with Drama at Leeds. University was fun but not too serious. After Anthony finished the degree he forgot about money. He wanted to write plays. His father wanted him to get a proper job. Something with a career plan and a pension. Playwright seemed impossible. There were no playwrights in Llanelli. Surely he could write plays in his spare time. The Llanelli Players were always looking for new people.

Anthony forced his way through a series of grim restaurant jobs until he was finally made assistant manager at Pizza Express. He had been good at it. His father saw hope in the title of Assistant Manager. Anthony was now in the restaurant business. When he visited his mother in Llanelli, people still asked him how the restaurant business was going.

He met Jac at Pizza Express. They had both been serving tables, sharing the tips. One night after work they ended up back at his dreary flat off Cowbridge Road. They opened a bottle of Mesquite. Jac had stayed. He wanted to know what Anthony was going to do. Anthony showed him his work.

Jac forced him to request an interview with the literary manager of the Sherman Theatre. It had a reputation for new plays. He had sent a play in six months previously but had received no reply. The literary manager was a thin uninspired man in his early thirties. He flirted hopelessly, almost desperately, with Anthony. A week later they offered him a contract of production. Sometimes you simply had to stand up for yourself. It seemed a long time ago. Anthony knew Jac had changed his life.

His father had never really accepted Jac. He was civil but cold. It was all a bit beyond his experience. He had wanted grandchildren. Anthony was his only child. Anthony didn't hold it against him. His father was a good man. There were a lot of people at his funeral.

Then there were six years of each other. Their own world.

The money had come as a surprise. The unexpected rush of it. His first commissioned play was worth six thousand pounds. He had lived for a year and a half on the money. Now in Asilah he was embarrassed by it. He had recently bought himself a new car. A Volkswagen Beetle with huge headlamps that looked like eyes. He looked at the car in a way that unnerved him, the sixteen thousand pounds of shine, curves and metal transferring itself into an expression of his wealth and well-being. He'd heard Jac's new boyfriend drove an Astra. This knowledge gave him a perverse enjoyment he was deeply worried by.

The bus had passed men on the side of the road. They were riding donkeys or herding goats. They didn't seem as if they could be part of the same world.

They arrived in Chefchaouen in the late afternoon. It was a town trapped at the blind head of a valley. The mountains continued up into the clouds beyond the blue terraced streets. His hotel was optimistically called The Parador. It had a swimming pool that was tacked onto a slope beyond the garden with a view down into the valley. But a thin mist drifted down from the mountains and no one used it. Anthony shared the breakfast room each morning with a party of Americans. They were old but seemed healthy with fine skin and bones carrying them well into their seventies. They talked to each other but ignored Anthony. He attempted to start a conversation each morning but was met with only polite short replies.

The town reminded him of a hill station he had visited for a week in India. It had the same narrow, terraced streets. But here there was more space, fewer people. He was offered more mint tea and a lot of grass. Most of the young Westerners seemed to be here for the marijuana. He had avoided it in college. It was a type

139

of penance he was happy with. Jac had sometimes brought some home, and they smoked it late at night with the windows open, listening to the sounds of the city at night. He always felt slightly ridiculous smoking. The unusual touch of the rolled paper filled with dried plants. He liked the smell better. The sweet promise of it. But here he refused the offers.

He bought more things he didn't need, copper bangles, postcards, odd-looking wooden boxes that reminded him of cuckoo clocks without the bird. He was reduced to giving some away to the children who accosted him for money. The begging here was only half serious. Here the children had homes to go back to.

He met the man from the bank for tea. The visit was going well for him. He had finished the training and had a day spare to be a tourist.

'Sometimes it is good to have nothing to do. Just to be? Don't you think?'

After three days he caught another bus back down to the coast at Asilah. It had an appealing write-up in his *Lonely Planet* guide, although no mention in *Spartacus*. He wrote another postcard to Jac but didn't post it. He found a hotel on the sea front. Huge blue waves rushed in across a wide open beach. He could feel the sea in the air and the history in the stones of the old town. Portuguese, British, Spanish and French had all fought over this piece of the world. He had often stayed in places where the

Portuguese had built forts. They had a lovely way with stones and the sea. The town had charm. Tree-lined boulevards backing away from a promenade lined with restaurants that served fine French coffee.

He spent a day on the beach. He was resisting the urge to check his email account. He was hoping Jac had written but was afraid he had not. It was a couple of weeks now. He had come to see him off on Cardiff station. It was as if he were performing some last duty. A final leaving. Jac had taken a day off from the new Coffee Republic he was managing. Anthony couldn't believe how miserable he felt. He had watched Jac from the train. He could see Jac's relief, as if he had become a burden. The whole thing had become a burden. The expectations of happiness. Maybe he wasn't meant to be happy.

A group of students were playing football on the beach. A sharp wind blew in off the water, but the players seemed to be able to tease the ball between them, as if it were an object of their own will. They were all lithe men who moved with a grace that was beautiful.

The ease with which he could remove himself from his world caught him. The money he had at home was enough. Here it seemed like too much. He thought about Rashid. The first night in a new country, a strange new man. He had been waiting for him at the top of the alleyway. He was more composed. His suit pulled tight around him. He could sense he wanted more.

'Maybe we can walk together?'

He had taken him back to the hotel.

'No one will know you.'

It hadn't taken long in the room. He was young, inexperienced, still scared. Anthony had brought his own condoms. Rashid's skin was rather beautiful, brown and tight across his chest, his buttocks small, feeling full in his hands. Anthony felt desire even as he was thinking of Jac. Rashid lay on the bed afterwards covered in the smells of sex, smiling, open. Anthony felt the guilt swallow him again. He walked into the bathroom, closed the door, took a shower. When he returned to the room Rashid was dressed.

'You want me to go?'

'It is probably best.'

His face lost its hopefulness.

'Wait, I will give you something.' Anthony reached for his trousers on the floor. He took out his wallet. As he offered Rashid fifty euros he felt the sting of his hand sharp across his face.

'I am not your boy.' He spat at his feet and left.

In the afternoon he returned to his hotel room. He made love to Jac's memory, the white, starched sheets sharp and exciting on his own skin. It was a relief to come on his own, without any guilt. He fell asleep into the deep heat of the afternoon. The music of God woke him. It was a beautiful sound. He began to cry.

Richard Lewis Davies is a writer and publisher. His work includes novels, plays, poetry and essays. His fiction includes the novels *Work, Sex and Rugby*, *Tree of Crows* and *My Piece of Happiness*. He is also a playwright with productions including *Football* and *Spinning the Round Table* both touring UK wide with several Theatre Wales nominations for best new work. His play *Sex and Power at the Beau Rivage* about the meeting of Rhys Davies and D.H Lawrence in the French Mediterranean of Bandol was produced by Theatr Y Byd and also toured nationally. His travel book *Freeways* won the John Morgan Award. He won the Rhys Davies short story award for his story 'Mr Roopratna's Chocolate' and he has recently been writing a series of books for children entitled *Tai and the Tremorfa Troll*.

The story 'We Were Winning' was commissioned by the Equality and Human Rights Commission to mark the 60th anniversary of the Universal Declaration of Human Rights. For more information go to www.equalityhumanrights.com

PARTHIAN

Award-winning
Welsh Writing

www.parthianbooks.co.uk